The Fog Within

By

Nick Shamhart

Dedication

This book is for my daughter Paige. She is severely autistic, mentally handicapped, and a true shining example of the word unique. She is unlike anyone I have ever met, unlike anyone I am likely to meet, and she has changed my life forever. I've never hidden the fact of her malady from the world. If anything I've done as much as I can to talk about her condition publicly and often. I share anecdotes and stories, when and where I can, so other parents going through what my wife and I are living with, dealing with, and doing our best to survive (sanity marginally intact) may not feel so alone and frustrated. Sharing our personal life in stories I tell at Q&As and book signings, plus what I post about online, has constantly piqued people's curiosity. They have asked me for years, when will I write a book about autism? To be honest, I never wanted to. It was never a thought or desire. Even with all the goofy things my Paige does, it was never, ever, something I wanted to do. I live with autism every day, and writing, well that has been my refuge from autism. Writing was the place I could go when the world around me seemed to make little to no sense. I could retreat into a world I created, a world that did make sense. My books.

I realized what I was doing; my retreat into writing, whether unintentional or on purpose, was not that far from a controlled form of autism. I'm not saying I was, or am, autistic. I'm not the spokesperson any cause would want as their champion. I only mean to say that I could identify with that desire to withdraw from the world around me as many autistics do.

That identification let me realize I did have an autism story to tell. Not a how-to non-fiction advice book that claims I have the answer! (Because I don't folks, there are no answers to life. What we so blithely term life is complex and really all a matter of mind – or mind versus genetics and survival mechanisms to be specific. So why should something as complex as mental illness, something incorrect or ill within our troglodytic definitions of the word mind, have answers when life alone - not mentally ill-life - leaves the best of us stumped?) I also didn't want to write some fictional story that simply has a character with autism (typically one that has super savant powers. My Paige can scoot across the length of our house like a dog scratching its butt on the grass in less than a minute, but I doubt that's much of a savant power. It's cool. I can't do it, trust me I've tried, but it's not savant-worthy). I feel the savant character has been overdone in all forms of entertainment.

No, this story is about everything my daughter Paige has taught me. It is told from what I have learned - what life has given me as a crash-course really - about autism and the day to day life of someone who retreats, not because they want to as I do with my writing, but because something has made it so they do. Be it genetics, environmental, behavioral, or who knows what, the list is endless, but the end result is the same: a person who sees the world differently, and not through the lens of cultural norms the rest of us do.

Paige has taught me so much about life. She has shown me what it means to be human, to be a spirit, a mind, a body (not always working in concert), to be a person. She has shown me what others are capable of, from the cruel to the kind. She has taught me that a person can cling to another for comfort in a storm only one of them sees and feels, that a single embrace can say more than the works of a million poets.

......And here is the hardest, saddest part of my dedication. I have failed her. I will always believe that of myself. No matter to what extent everyone else sees us: physicians, psychiatrists, teachers, therapists, friends, family, and simply the world, I will never feel as if I have succeeded, despite how much she has taught and shown me. If one day my little girl can read this ... if one day you can read this, Paige, and you understand what Daddy has said, and that you think he showed the world just the smallest bit of what you've shown him, what it really means to be human, what really matters and what does not, then maybe on that day little one, Daddy will have succeeded.

Acknowledgements

For all the love and support of my readers, for all the help from my proofreaders, for all the patience from my editors, for all those who love a good run-on sentence, for every parent dealing with any type of special needs child, for every parent period, for every child that sees the world differently, for every child who sees others being cruel and steps in to be kind, for compassion, for humanity, for doctors who care more for patients than money, for charity, for kindness, for all those things and more this book was written. Thank you.

Author's Notes I

I want to clarify upfront that *The Fog Within* is not a biographical work on my autistic daughter. It is a work of fiction. As I write this she is still completely non-verbal, so I won't pretend that she has somehow communicated these concepts to me through the use of sign language or a computer picture recognition system of speech. I would not mislead you like that. I have for years tried to explain my daughter's condition through the analogy that she was and is lost in a fog. That seemed to me to be the most relatable explanation for people – an idea they could picture better than the culturally abused diagnosis of *autism*. That is how I decided upon this approach, this perhaps anthropomorphized, yet I feel realistic expression of a mind trapped under a medical umbrella, a spectrum, to toss out an overused and all but meaningless term. I don't mean for you to interpret a negative connotation when I say anthropomorphized. I don't mean to say that my daughter or other people with autism do not have the same human characteristics that non-autistics do. It is simply that those who do not have experience with the mentally handicapped may construe their behaviors as so alien at times that to ascribe our general vernacular and thoughts onto them may seem like a stretch at best - if not an outright elaboration. But trust me, a man who has spent years around the mentally handicapped … nothing is a stretch. You can see it all in their eyes: the pain, the frustration, the anger, the sadness, the joy, the hope. It's all there. You just need to take the time to step outside yourself and see it.

So please, though some aspects of this story may ring with familiarity to those that have followed my career when I speak about my daughter, remember the characters are not my family and I. They are an amalgam of my experiences with the world of autism in the forms of: doctors, therapists, schools, other afflicted families, and society as a whole in how the system works or does not work … as the case may be.

How we help those who cannot help themselves is the moral measure of any society.

I wanted to write a story that is Young Adult, or YA as the publishing industry deems it, in the classic sense of the word. Perhaps something, without over stating my literary value, in the footsteps of the greats Judy Blume, Cynthia Voigt, and Roald Dahl. A story that deals with what it's like for a classic young adult. Not a late teen or early twenty-something dealing with a whole different set of cultural issues, mainly adapting to said culture's mores. I wanted to focus on the idea that a child may be so incapacitated that those concepts of *fitting in* were more of a dream than a standard measure of daily living. With that in mind, please notice that tense contradictions and inappropriate word choices in this story are not typos or poor writing. They are intentional because I do not see a young person afflicted with any mental illness feeling the need to keep to the proper rules of grammar. I find it a tragic sign of the times that I feel the need to address that at all. But the world has turned critical to a fault, to a point where I want to stress that the protagonist of this story is mentally handicapped. Fragmented, run on, and simple sentences would be the least of her concerns when she tries to tell you her story. No one knows how a blind person perceives an object through touch. No one knows how a mute would tell a story. The story is narrated by a young girl with autism, so she can tell "her" story and not as some distant third person narrative. I wanted to write a book that may or may not help both young adults … and their older contemporaries … see, feel, hear, and experience what life can be like for a person with a mental handicap, to perhaps pull an increasingly apathetic world out of their careless bubbles and see life through someone else's eyes for once. Maybe, just maybe, empathize instead of criticize and judge … maybe.

~ Nick Shamhart

Part I:

Childhood

The Fog Within

Chapter One

They tell me the fog isn't real, that it's all in my head, but they don't see it, they don't feel it, they don't touch it, or smell it, or taste it, or hear it. That's what it's like to have the fog. The fog does all those things back to me and more. I can't tell them it's a fog, because it isn't really a fog. It's light and dark, thick and thin, loud and quiet, smelly and dull, happy and sad. It's all kinds of things, but fog seems to be the best name I have for it. It sweeps in uncontrolled and unwanted, just like any type of weather ... but fog hides things. Fog keeps you from seeing and in return it keeps things from seeing you. It's easy to get lost in a fog. That's why I call it a fog ... I get lost in it a lot.

They call it *autism*. I don't understand that. How does *autism* explain smiling at your daddy sitting next to you on the couch one minute, and then the fog rolls in and you don't see him anymore? You see dark scary blurs. Daddy pops in and out of focus, but the blurs crowd him out, shoving him away. You push at the fog, you reach out to get Daddy's attention, but the fog settles in and you scream. The fog can do so many things. What's autism? Just another word they say around me. When I was four and my parents were so upset about the fog, they said autism so much I started to think it was a new name for me, "Hi, I'm Megan Autism. Nice to meet you." Only I can't say that. Not with my mouth anyway. I tried and tried for years. I'd tell everybody around me all sorts of things. What I liked to do, what my favorite foods were, what cartoons I liked to watch, but the fog always took those words away. The fog made it so my voice was lost or unintelligible to other people. That's one more reason I hate the fog; it takes so much away from me.

My name is Megan Cooper and my parents tell me that I'm eleven. They said ten a lot for a while and nine before that. I like numbers. The fog can pull me away from numbers or distort them sometimes, but when I come out of the fog the numbers are still there. Daddy says, "Megan is eleven years old." I think years have to do with the sun and the ground? Or the earth? Earth the big ball in space not the dirt from the garden. Too many names for too many things. The fog loves to blur words and names. Names are just words too - confusing. I'm in the fifth grade. I like five. Five is an awesome number! Five days in a school week! I like school, but the fog doesn't. No, the fog hates school. The fog makes it hard to wait in line for anything and there's too much waiting at school. I'll be okay for a few minutes, but if the lunch line is too long, the fog rolls in. It pushes at my ears and makes me cover them. The fog makes my hands shake and twitch because I'm stuck in one spot and I can't move. I want to run. I don't care where, just run, really, really fast. I no longer want lunch. I want to move, because the fog has taken away my appetite, too. The other kids don't understand the fog, so when I fight it they stare at me. Some call me names. I think they're being mean, but sometimes it's hard to tell. Other kids, my friends, are why I like to go to school. Five days a week - Five!

I've been to a lot of different schools. Some were big like shopping malls and some were small like somebody's house. I didn't realize there were so many schools at first. Daddy would just say, "Time for school, Megan," and we'd go. I thought that the school I went to was the only one. That was *school* like how you get pizza from *the* pizza place. Then I found out there were different pizza places too! It gets confusing. I remember thinking that my first school was where everybody went, so school was school. I was scared for a while. The fog was even worse when I was little. When I was in preschool, whatever that means. When I was three, four, and five! Five! It was bad then. The fog wasn't the fog then. I didn't have anything to relate it to. I didn't have a name for it. It was just sounds and sights that hurt or helped. I was scared most of the time, or really happy with whatever it was I found interesting. I can't remember what those things were now – the fog lives with me and has a name, so I know the fog is blurring those memories. I didn't realize other people weren't seeing and hearing the fog too until I went to school. I figured the whole world was like me ... scared.

"Megan honey, it's time for school! Wake up." That's Daddy.

I can hear him calling from the kitchen. I don't want to get out of bed this morning. The fog woke me up in the middle of the night. It does that a lot. The fog screams or whistles or whispers at me, and I wake up while everybody else is asleep. It's harder some days than others. It was really bad when I was little, around three, four, or five. Five! That was when I'd wake up and Mommy or Daddy would try to talk to me, but the fog was there, and thick too, so it was hard to hear them and impossible for them to hear me. They'd yell a lot, but I didn't understand why. I didn't know the fog wasn't waking them up too. I didn't know that everybody else was sleeping and that my yelling or laughing or jumping was waking them up. So why be mad at me? Be mad at the fog. I hate the fog.

"Megan? Come on MC, I know you can hear me!" Daddy again, but I ignore him.

I just want to stay here, squished under my bed. Not asleep but sleepy, warm and snuggly. That helps shut the fog up sometimes so I can get back to sleep. I yank my mattress off my bed, pile all my pillows and blankets on top, and then squeeze under the whole mess. It squishes me into the carpet and if I'm lucky all that stuff pressing down will drown out the fog, and help me fall back to sleep. If not, I flip through some books or magazines, jump up and down, tap on my walls, and try anything I can to wring away the extra energy the fog leaves me with when it won't let me fall back to sleep.

"Come on MC! It's *Hammer Time*! Let's move it!" That's Daddy coming down the hall. I can hear his voice getting louder as he gets closer to my room.

He calls me all kinds of weird names that I don't understand most of the time. I thought that was the fog messing with me for a while, but then I realized he's just weird. I like Daddy. He tries to understand the fog more than anybody else. He gets mad or sad sometimes about it, but he always tries to help first. It's when the fog pushes him away, and I don't want it to, that things are the worst. I can see it in his eyes. They're sad and tired. I want him to help, and he wants to help, but the fog keeps us apart, keeps us from helping each other.

The weight of the mattress goes away and I turn my head to see Daddy and his tired eyes looking at me. He leans down and says, "Rough night, huh? Big party?"

I groan and roll over, pulling a pillow over my head. Daddy pulls the pillow away and says, "Hey, you're not getting any sympathy out of me, kiddo. I didn't get invited to the party, so up, up, up!" and he tugs on my ankle gently so I slide out from under the mattress before he lets it drop back to the carpet with a loud whump sound. Daddy is big. Sometimes when the fog is real bad he has to hold my arms at my sides so the fog doesn't make me hurt myself. I've had cuts and bruises when other people try to do it, but Daddy is big and he holds on tight. That can either make the fog stop early or it makes the fog angry and things get worse. If I'm not trapped by just the fog, but restrained and can't move, I get angrier and that just makes the fog worse. The fog feeds off of the anger and things get worse and worse. This morning I don't fight Daddy as he helps me get dressed. I just groan and growl at him to make sure he knows I'm not happy about getting up. He nods, saying, "Yeah yeah, I feel you. I hate mornings too, but you got to get up and go to school, so I have to get up and take you. I did my groaning half an hour ago when I kept hitting the snooze button."

Daddy understands me, but he talks too much. I only catch about half of what he says, maybe less … and sometimes I only pretend that I don't understand. Mommy says it's me being stubborn like Daddy, but I think of it as payback for things like dragging me out of bed. Dressed, I wander after Daddy as he heads back toward the kitchen, but I don't go all the way with him. I flop on the couch, and while I hear him getting me a plate of something that I'm not going to eat, I bury myself in the couch cushions. I can hear Daddy put the plate of food on the table, but I don't move. I count in my head: one, two, three, four – "Megan, come on! Get your butt out here and eat. We have to leave for school in ten minutes!"

He didn't let me get to five, so I'm going to start over: one, two, three, four – "Megan for Christ's sake get up!"

Fine. I get up and wander out to the kitchen, groaning as I sit and lean my elbows on the table. I look down at the plate and groan louder. Yep, I'm not eating that. I grab a sip of juice, but push the plate with all the weird foods away. Two hours from now I know I'll want to eat. I'd scarf down everything on that plate, but right now it looks like butt. Smelly, gross butt that I'm not going to eat. I want some coffee and a cookie. Daddy has his back to me, so I make my noise for Daddy. I've tried to say, "Dad," but the fog won't let it come out, so, "Dat," is the best I can do. I use it for every adult, but Daddy knows when I mean him. He can hear the difference. To his back I yell, "Dat!"

"What?" he says, not turning around from what he's doing.

"Dat!" I say again, several times until he finally stops doing whatever he was doing and pays attention to me. Closing his computer he turns around, rolling his eyes, and asks, "What Megan? What can I do for you your highness?"

See, too many words. I use some signs. I know they aren't what everybody, my teachers, my aides, my therapists, my doctors, and all the other adult people I have to go see, think of as real words. But, the fog doesn't give me much time to focus, so I make do with what I can. I sign, cupping and moving one hand in the palm of my other for *cookie*. Then I twirl my fist for *coffee*. Daddy sighs; he knows what I asked for. I do the signs again. Daddy sighs again. I growl. Daddy sighs and says, "Fine! Fuck it, the doctors can bitch at me for giving you coffee, but they only get to see you for ten minutes every other month. I have to live with you. 'The caffeine will exacerbate her hyperactivity Mr. Cooper.' No shit Dr. Sherlock. Did it take four years of med school for you to figure that one out, or was it during your residency that the idea of caffeine being a stimulant really sank in? Giving her a half a cup of coffee is like throwing a ball for a dog. It's going to run around yapping and barking anyway. What hell is a little extra running and yapping going to hurt? I tell you Megan, people are so damn dense and ....."

He keeps on going. I don't have a clue what he's talking about, but I do know I'm getting my cookie and my coffee, so he can keep on going if it makes him feel better. He keeps on talking even after he takes away the plate of butt and replaces it with three cookies and a mug of coffee. I eat the filling out of all three and start to eat the cookie disks from two, but then I remember to dip them in my coffee like I saw other people do. I finish off half the cookie disks before the fog starts to edge in. It's not a big

17

storm this time, but a quiet little whisper that suggests that the cookie disks once dunked in the coffee make a really cool paste. A paste that could be used to color on the table with. I start to make squiggly lines: one, two, three, four, five! But before I can make a sixth squiggle Daddy notices and wipes my hands off with a wet washrag, saying, "Oh look, if you're painting then you must be full. I guess if you don't want to eat anymore. It's time for school."

At least he let me get to five that time.

Chapter Two

The ride to school is fun. I like listening to the radio. It makes me bounce around if it's a song I really like. Daddy plays all kinds of different music. Sometimes it's kind of loud with guitars and people who sound like they're mad and yelling instead of singing. Sometimes it's just instruments. I like it best when it's one of the songs that they play on the movies I watch. It makes me think of the movie and I can escape into the images. Escape is the key to avoiding the fog. I can dodge the fog sometimes if I feel it rolling in and I switch my mind over real fast to a movie scene or a song I like. Music helps with the fog. I don't really like the only instrument stuff. Daddy and other people like my teachers, that aren't teachers, too many names for things, therapists or teachers, adults, grown-ups, bigger than me, too many names, but they call the instrument stuff calming or relaxing. I call it boring. I want to move. I want to hear somebody else's voice. I don't understand what they are singing about most of the time. It sounds like mumbling, but I like to hear the voice anyway. It's like an anchor in the fog that I can grab ahold of ... sometimes, if I'm lucky. Nothing works every time. The fog won't let it. The fog is too strong. Megan is too weak. I wish I was strong like Daddy. Daddy wouldn't let the fog bother him. He'd wave his big hands and arms and make the fog go away. Swish, poof, and gone, leave me alone fog. I wish he could do that for my fog.

I like to sing along with the music. It may not sound like singing to you. But in my head it does. In my head all the noises I make sound like words. The noises sound just like the music on the radio. Even Daddy has trouble with the noises sometimes. He says he has to see my face before he knows if it's a happy noise or a mad noise. I've tried to tell him that it isn't a happy noise at all. That it's me singing, but, all that comes out are gibberish sounds, "Bazumba," or "Pissum-pissum," I know those aren't words, that the fog won't let words come out, but sometimes I just have to try anyway.

When we get to school Daddy walks me to the door. I like to skip and run whenever I can, walking is just so boring. Walking is like that instrument music - boring. It's easy to forget what I was supposed to be doing when I'm skipping or running. Daddy holds my hand. He says, "Megan, you have to watch for cars."

I see cars everywhere. I don't know why I'm supposed to watch for them. There are cars all over the place. There are cars parked by the school, driving down the road, parked in driveways, everywhere - moving fast, moving slow. I see: one, two, three, four–

"Come on, MC. We're twenty minutes late as it is," Daddy says as he pulls on my arm. Twenty, sheesh, who cares about twenty? I was almost to five. Five!

My teacher grown-up person meets Daddy at the school doorway. I'm already thinking about what I'm going to do when I get to the classroom, so I give Daddy a distracted kiss and take the teacher's hand. Sometimes I look back to see if Daddy is still there, but most of the time the fog keeps me distracted … and I forget. Not about Daddy, but about everything other than what I'm doing.

I like the teacher; she's nice. I think she has a name like Megan or Daddy or Mommy, but names are hard to remember. It's not just the fog. People talk fast – especially Mommy, my teachers, and other little kids, fast, fast, fast. They talk like I'm not there a lot. It's okay, because sometimes I'm not. The fog pulls me away so I miss what they're saying, or I'm just not listening because what they are saying is boring like walking and instrument music. People, especially teacher people, talk two ways around me. They talk to me in really happy voices, "Megan, it's so good to see you! Are you happy to be at school today?" Sometimes I am and I try to say something, but they don't understand, so I giggle or laugh – everybody understands laughing. Laughing is my best way to let people know I'm happy. Other times I don't want to be there. I growl when they ask me if I'm happy. Growling and grinding my teeth work pretty good to let people know that, no, I am not happy. The other way people talk is as if I'm not there. They talk over my head, not just because I'm short; they talk with bigger words and talk fast so I can't follow. That's when they say each other's names a lot. I figure if they aren't talking to me, then I don't need to try and fight the fog to remember their names.

When I get to my room I take my jacket off and drop it on the floor near my locker, cubbyhole, place where I put my things. Teacher says, "Megan, pick that up and put it on the hook please."

Growl, fine, I do it, but I growl. Who cares if my jacket is on a hook or on the floor? I know where I left it and when I want to put it back on to go outside then that's where it will be, sheesh. Grown-up people have all kinds of weird rules and ideas like that. I don't understand them. I think, hey the fog isn't making me scream right now, I'm happy, why are we messing around with jackets and hooks – let's do something! But grown-ups love their stupid, weird rules and really get grumpy if you don't follow them. I fight those rules a lot, but sometimes I just give in because it's easier to get what I want if I do it their silly way.

I sit at my desk and everybody kind of does what the boss teacher asks. I don't know her name either, but the other teacher people look to her, and follow what she does, so I guess she's the boss. My friends... I ...I'm sorry. I don't know their names either. I want to. There's a girl with long brown hair.

She smiles a lot and rocks in place. She lets me play with her hair. It smells nice like flowers. I like to smell people's hair. That really upsets some people and others think it's funny. I wish that I could think of her name. What is long brown haired girl's name? I try to think of her name. I do. I look at her and I yell at myself, "Megan, you know her name! Now think, what is it? She's nice you should know her name!"

But I can't. That makes me mad at myself and sad. She's nice. I know that I know her name, but it won't come to mind. I should, oh no, when I get upset, it's harder to fight the fog. It's like tripping over something. You can feel yourself falling and you move your arms around, trying to keep your balance ... but, you fall anyway. I'm too mad at myself for not remembering her name that the fog sweeps in. I can't fight it. I start to growl to let the teacher people know I can't help it. The fog is pushing. They don't notice at first. I growl louder as I lose more control. Boss teacher says, "Megan, please be quiet. We're working on the letter H."

It's too late though. I can't hear her. I can barely see her through the fog. It...

...Mad, wring fingers, mad, angry, stupid Megan! Stupid! Why can't you! Faces come into view. Daddy? Daddy what are you doing here? Wait, he's gone. Daddy? Someone tries to stop me, but, pull hair, pull hair, ouch, pain! Pain! Pain!

The Fog Within

Focus pain...red, red, and smell bitter, sour, gross, sharp smell. Stop don't like it! Get it away! Want to stop. Want Daddy...or Mommy? Where's Mommy! Hurts...

...Then the fog leaves me alone – poof! I'm sitting at my desk in control again. Teachers are upset. They are talking over me, about me. I don't care the fog is gone! People, the fog is gone! Look, Megan is smiling, laughing, happy, let's do something. How about food? I'm hungry. I knew I should have eaten that plate of food Daddy gave me, but I didn't want it then. I want it now. Teacher people are still talking over me when I make my "dat" noise to get their attention ... oh well, fine, I'll just go get my food. I know where it is. It's in a pink bag Daddy puts in my bigger bag. Why two bags? Small bag in big bag? Grown-ups are weird. I walk over to my cubbyhole thing and start to open my bag, but boss teacher says, "Megan, it isn't snack time yet. Come back over to your desk so we can do some coloring."

Snack? More names. I don't understand grown-ups and their names. It's not lunch yet Megan, or snack, or dinner, or supper. I'm hungry. I eat. It's simple. Why do grown-ups have to complicate everything with words and ideas? I see people eat all the time outside, inside, at stores, on street corners, and in parks. Why is it snack for them, or lunch, or dinner, and not me? Why do I have set times to eat? That's stupid. I mean really stupid. Ticking black lines on the round white thing by the door tell us when I can eat or glowing numbers on those black box things. It's fun to play with those numbers in my head, but I don't want those numbers playing with me. The numbers shouldn't say when I can eat my stupid snack. They're just numbers – they don't eat. I want the cookie out of my bag, now!

I can feel the fog waiting to sweep back in. I have to think is it worth the cookie Megan to shove yourself back into the fog? No, it's close, I want the stupid cookie, so it's real close, but I go back and sit at my desk and wait for the stupid ticking bars to tell the teacher it's time for me to have my cookie. Stupid ticking bars.

Chapter Three

Recess, I don't like it. No, not one little bit. That has been a problem at every school I've ever gone to. It's like the whole meals thing. Now, it's time to eat. Now, it's time to play. Who says? The sun, Daddy, teacher, the fog? When you want to play, you should play, right? No, no, no, no, not if the grown-ups have anything to say about it ... and, of course, they will. They have something to say about everything. They never shut up. They talk and talk and talk. I hope one day the fog goes away so far that I can look around at all the grown-ups babbling away nonstop and finally say, "Shut up!"

I'd probably get yelled at for it, too. Even though it would be words like everybody wants me to use. But Daddy wouldn't yell at me for that though. Daddy told me once he didn't care what I said. He said I could say some really bad words and that would be all right with him. If I could say anything he'd be happy. What makes a word bad? It didn't do anything wrong. It's a word. I don't like dogs; does that make dog a bad word? I bet it's more stupid grown-up stuff, like recess and lunch - bad words, good words ... sheesh.

Lunch comes after recess at my school. I have to stand around outside and wait to eat even longer. Stupid waiting, that's a grown-up idea if there ever was one. I don't play with the other kids like brown haired girl. Think Megan, you can remember her name! No, I can't. I wish I could, but it's just not there. I don't play though. Not like everybody else does. When I was younger three, four, five - Five! I used to play. I'd run around, go up and down the slide, and just yell and laugh. When you're little the other kids don't mind the fog as much. They run around laughing and yelling and so do you. It's what little kids do. My little brother does it all the time. But now that I'm older and the other kids play games with rules and balls, or sit around talking and giggling, I don't play. I don't understand what they're doing. I can throw a ball. It's easy. Pick up ball, throw to friend, friend throws back and you catch it, okay, done, game over. Why does it keep on going? Why is that fun?

So while I wait for lunch, stupid waiting, I walk back and forth along the school, running my fingers against the bricks. The rough, prickly sensation gives me something to focus on. It feels weird after a while. My fingers go numb and if I take them away from the bricks it feels like they are still touching the wall, still tingling. I like that. It makes me think the fog isn't so strange. If I can feel like I'm touching the wall, even though I'm not, maybe seeing things that aren't there or hearing things that aren't there isn't so strange. Running my fingers along the wall is a way to control the fog … for a while anyhow.

The Fog Within

The teachers come out and watch us at recess, some do on certain days and other teachers do on different ones. I don't know if they take turns watching us like they make me do with my computer. I don't like to take turns. Taking turns is stupid because grown-ups always toss that dumb clock thing into it again. Megan you had your turn for ten minutes, now it's Sally's. Hey, Sally! That's brown haired girl's name! I'm glad I remembered that. It makes me smile. But sharing by the grown-up way is dumb, ticking black lines on a circle tell you when your turn is over? Sometimes I think grown-ups only follow their rules because they don't have the fog messing with them. If they didn't know when or where the fog was going to yank them away from their friends or family and how long they would be lost in the fog, I think they'd throw every one of those ticking clock things out the window. I sometimes throw things I don't like out of windows, or, if it's a spoon, I'll throw it into the woods behind our house. I hate spoons! Daddy says I'm supposed to stay in the yard, so if somebody brings a spoon into the house, I take it out back and throw it into the woods as hard and as far as I can.

At school I have to ignore the spoons. It's really hard to do. The teachers call it tolerating. They say, "Megan, you're tolerating the spoons in the cafeteria very well this year."

Two years ago the fog swept in and I ran around the cafeteria collecting every spoon in a bucket and I tossed them out the window. It felt good, but I got in trouble for it. The school called Daddy and he came and talked over me to the really important teacher. What's she called? ... the principal! Hey, I'm doing good today. Daddy talked to the principal. She's nice, she laughed and Daddy laughed and I laughed, but Daddy said I had to leave the school spoons alone. They were different spoons. Not true. Spoons are spoons, but Daddy looked serious so I've tried real hard, even though every lunch those spoons clink and clack and click on the trays and bowls. They make me want to scream ... but I've been good.

The bell rings. Loud. I don't like the bell. I kind of do because it means I can go inside for lunch, but I don't like how loud it is. The teachers who are out with us today (I think when they take turns they're eating their lunch first and they just don't want us to know about it) tell us to line up and go inside, slowly. No running, never running when it makes sense. Don't run to go get your food because you are hungry, but go ahead and run after the ball outside. It's okay to run outside but not inside. Weird grown-up rules.

Sometimes, like today, when I've eaten the food Daddy packs for me before the time I'm supposed to, rules blah, I go with my teacher and have a lunch on a tray. Tray lunches can be good or gross. I'm hoping today's isn't gross, because I'm still hungry. I like food. I like to touch it, squish it, eat it, taste it,

29

pull it out after I've chewed on it to see what it looks like all browns, tans, and mushy. Food is fun. The teachers don't let me pick out my tray lunch like the other kids do. The other kids put one brownie or cookie on their tray, and a sandwich, and one carton of milk. They tried letting me do that once and when I piled everything I wanted onto a tray, they had to call Daddy again. What's wrong with twenty brownies and one fruit cup? I left plenty of fruit cups for the other kids. So, they pick something out for me and hope that I'll eat it instead.

I got lucky. Today my teacher brought me meatloaf. I like that. It's fun to pull it into pieces and then dip the pieces in dippy white stuff. Daddy says, "Ranch dressing." More words with more weird meanings. Can't a word just mean one thing like my name? Megan means me. I thought ranches were where horses lived and dressing was that soft bread mush that comes out of turkey butts. I still like it whatever it's called. I like to dip foods into other foods. One of the teachers not teachers … therapist … says dipping things works on some big word. What does she call it? Manual dexti-something. I don't know, more words, dipping is fun, if the grown-ups are okay with it and don't have some stupid no dipping clock ticking rule, then I don't care!

After lunch the rest of my day at school drags on. I mean ooonnnnnn. Back in the room the fog threatens to pull me in as the day takes forever to be done. Some days I make it to the end fog-free and others I lose it after lunch, waiting, and waiting, and waiting. School is too long for the fog, and too long for me. If we didn't have to wait all the time for the stupid ticking black bars on the round white circle, and just did stuff when we felt like it, school would be over in half the time.

Today was a good day, not just because of meatloaf, but I made it to the end of the day with the fog pulling me away only once. At school one heavy trip into the fog means a good day. My teacher walks me to a different door at the end of the day when Daddy picks me up. Not the same door I went in, but a different door for going out. Whatever, more stupid grown-up rules, one door for in and one door for out? Okay, if it makes them happy, I can deal with it. It's weird if you ask me though. I can see Daddy through the glass waiting in the car. I get to the door and teacher lets me go out by myself. She says something but I'm already focused on Daddy. The fog doesn't like it when I focus ... but the weird thing is as long as the fog directs the focus, like if it wants me to turn a light switch on and off, over and over and over, it's okay with that. But if I want to focus on something or somebody, if it's something I want to do, I have to really work hard against the fog. It would be nice not to have to fight the fog and just walk around like everybody else.

Chapter Four

I fight through the fog to focus on Daddy. He gets out of the car to meet me halfway up the sidewalk and takes my hand to walk me back to the car. He smiles and takes my bag within bags from me. He helps me get in the car and asks for a kiss. I give him one. It's the easiest way I have to tell him I love him. I can't say that. The fog sticks in my throat and won't let the words come out, but I can give him a kiss. That's the best I can do like laughing to let people know I'm happy. I do love him too, because he'll ask me how my day was. He knows the fog won't let me answer, but he asks anyway. If I smile he knows it was a good day, or if I growl he knows it was a bad day. We start to drive away from the school and Daddy turns the radio back from boring music to songs with mumbled words. I like that too.

"Megan." That's not Daddy's voice. "Megan!" I turn to look next to me, where I hear the voice coming from. Sometimes the fog can make me hear things that aren't there, so I don't always respond right away. It's a way for the fog to play another mean trick. I think somebody is there and I look, but they aren't. Or worse yet, the fog makes me see somebody who isn't there. I don't like that, it scares me. It isn't the fog though, not this time. It's my younger brother Tahbey. He came with Daddy to pick me up from school. He does that sometimes.

His name isn't "Tahbey" it's Todd, but when Mommy and Daddy first brought Tahbey home they called him "Baby" for a long time. I thought his name was baby. "Be careful of the baby, Megan." "Watch out for the baby, Megan!" and on and on. Then they started calling him Todd after he learned to walk, so I call him Tahbey, combining Todd and baby, just to be safe. I can actually say, "Tahbey" like I say Dat for Daddy, that's part of why I say it that way too.

"Megan," Tahbey says again. I look at him. He's short - a lot shorter than me. He doesn't go to school yet. He hangs out with Daddy a lot. "Megan," he won't stop saying my name until I say either, "Tahbey" or "Hi." I can't say hi, so I say, "Tahbey." He laughs and claps his little hands when I say his name. I like Tahbey. He doesn't care about the fog. He doesn't understand the fog, but he doesn't care about it either. He doesn't talk about the fog when it makes me yell or makes me grab a spoon and throw it away. He laughs, claps, or watches what the fog makes me do. He doesn't try to tell me it's okay like the grown-ups do. He just hangs out with me … whether I want him to or not, so I usually just let him. It's easier than listening to him cry or worse having Daddy tell me to be nice to Tahbey because he loves me.

We listen to one, two, three, four … only four songs on the way home. Good, but not as good as five. Daddy gets Tahbey out of the car first, but I run around him on the sidewalk and beat him to the door. He shouts, "Hey! Megan!" But I don't listen to him complain, I go right inside and Daddy carries Tahbey the rest of the way in. Mommy's awake when we get home. I like Mommy too, but she sleeps during the day and comes out at night like a raccoon. We learned about raccoons at the zoo. I like the zoo, too. Some days Mommy is awake during the day and sometimes she isn't. I bet it's one of those weird grown-up things that only makes sense to them. Sometimes at night when the fog wakes me up I wonder if Mommy is awake too because Mommy and Daddy say she works at night. They tell me to do work at school. Work is coloring, or writing with a pencil, or using a computer to put together a puzzle, or other fun things. So, when I wake up I always hope Mommy's going to open my door and say, "Megan, want to help me work?" But she doesn't. Maybe someday she will. It would be nice to have somebody to be around when the fog wakes me up in the dark. I'm not scared of the dark or anything like Tahbey is; it's just lonely because the rest of the world is dark and everyone's asleep except me, Mommy, and the raccoons.

Mommy has food out for me most days when I get home. Food is fun. She has food out for Tahbey too, but we pick off of each other's plates and swap drinks back and forth. Mommy tried to get us to stop that for a while. We kept at it even though she said, "You two are going to share germs and rot your teeth and…" she kept going but I wasn't listening. It wasn't the fog, I just didn't care. Tahbey didn't either. He thinks whatever I have tastes better than what he has, so I eat the frosting off of all the cupcakes and brownies and then he takes the bottom cake stuff and eats that. He thinks it's good because I had it first, and I get to eat the better part, so we both are happy. Except for Mommy, but we don't care. Daddy says, "Just let them be, there are much worse things they could do. You have to fucking relax, honey." I don't know what he's talking about, but he must have said one of those bad words because Mommy starts talking to him, over me and Tahbey - loudly. We just keep on eating. I laugh. Tahbey laughs. Mommy and Daddy leave the room. I can still hear them talking over me in the kitchen, but they think if they aren't in the same room as me I won't know they are talking about me. Stupid grown-ups. I love them, but they are stupid most of the time.

It's nice to be home. At home the grown-up rules that don't make sense are a lot less than at school like Daddy not caring that Tahbey and I share food and drinks. Everybody is always telling everybody else to share, so what's the big problem? I tried sharing the other kids' food at school but the teachers got all upset and called Daddy. So, now I don't share at school. Unless it's for one of their stupid rules like sharing the computer, so it's good sharing as long as the sharing is done because grown-ups say so. If they don't then it's bad sharing? That's confusing, even without the fog I think that would confuse me.

Mommy and Daddy come out of the kitchen when they hear Tahbey yelling about something. I was flipping through a book, so I wasn't paying attention. I think Tahbey wandered down to his room and got stuck in his closet and couldn't get out because his yelling is kind of quiet. Daddy walks by and ruffles my hair. I hear him asking Tahbey, "What's wrong, buddy?" Daddy and his words; he calls everybody and everything by so many different words that other grown-ups can't follow him. I see it sometimes when he's talking to people and they're talking over me. Their eyes drift out of focus as they stare blankly at Daddy talking. I like that. It makes me feel better to know they don't understand what he says half the time either. Maybe some of them are fighting the fog too.

I was right, Tahbey had gotten stuck in his closet … again. He does that a lot. I think he just wants Daddy to go find him. Seconds later Tahbey runs out of his bedroom with Daddy chasing him. Daddy's hopping around like a giant frog making *ribbit* noises, flicking his tongue in and out like a frog, and saying, "I'm going to eat that little pest! Ribbit, ribbit, come here little boy." Tahbey falls to the floor and covers himself with pillows. He copied that from me. I like to lie under pillows, not on them. It's the pressure again like squeezing under my mattress. Tahbey giggles and squeals when Daddy uncovers him and starts tickling his feet. Tickling is fun. I toss my book aside and jump on Daddy's back so he'll wrestle and tickle with me too. He says, "Oh no, the little pest has a big friend. The two annoying bugs are trying to team up against the great and mighty frog. Our poor giant green-skinned hero! Whatever shall he do? Kermit was right, it's not easy at all!" Daddy's big, I've told you that before, but he is. He scoops Tahbey up under one arm like the boys playing with the brown ball at recess and with his other arm he reaches around, grabbing my waist and flips me forward, so he's holding both of us the same way. Tahbey is laughing and so am I. Daddy runs past Mommy where she's standing in the doorway still watching. He smiles at her, says, "Ribbit," then licks her face like a frog darting out his tongue. She laughs and wipes at her cheek as we go running past. Daddy races out the back door still carrying us and jumps onto the big trampoline we have in the backyard. I like the trampoline. I can bounce and bounce; both the fog and I like to bounce, so it's never a fight. Tahbey is still giggling and rolling around in a ball while Daddy tickles him. I start bouncing. Daddy sits up in a crouch and says, "This is how our great, green hero will foil the wicked, annoying, non-stop pests! He shall turn them from bugs who pester him into frogs! Presto change-o! Alakazam!" He swings his arms around like one of my friends in class who shakes a lot and rubbing both of our heads until our hair stands up on end, he says, "Turn these bugs into frogs!"

The Fog Within

I just laugh and jump up and down, but Tahbey starts crouching down like Daddy was earlier and making *ribbit* noises. They're happy, I'm happy, I don't know what Daddy is doing but we're all bouncing and laughing so I'm happy. We spend a long time out there bouncing, Daddy and Tahbey making frog noises and me jumping. Mommy eventually calls us in for dinner. She went and got pizza while we were out in the back yard. I like pizza - especially with a bowl of the dippy white stuff. I ate one, two, three pieces. I wanted to eat five. Five! But I was worried if I did I might throw up. I used to throw up a lot when I was little and both Mommy and Daddy would yell at me. Not every time, but only the times I would eat too much and start running around the living room. The fog makes me run a lot. It keeps me wanting to move, so running around the living room and down the hall to my room and back is a good way to keep the fog away. If I ate five, Five! pieces of pizza and went running, I'd start coughing and then throw up for sure. So I ate three. Not as good, but less mess and no yelling.

After dinner I know the day is almost over. It depends, sometimes it gets dark early. That happens when it's cold out, but if it's warm it gets dark later. That confuses me a lot. But I know when it's getting late that means two things: bath and movie! Movies are fun. When I was little, like Tahbey, Mommy and Daddy used to let me watch movies all day long, because I liked them so much, but I started to only want to watch part of a movie, because only part of it was good. That wasn't the fog that was just me. I only like the movies where it's drawings, cartoons? I don't like movies with real people. That scares me. Small people on a screen, what if they came out? I wouldn't mind it if the cartoons came out. I like them, but not all of them. Some movies are good enough they make more just like it only the cartoons do different things. There are other movies that the cartoons do different things but I only like the things they did the first time. They normally call those movies by their title and then a number after it. I've never seen a cartoon get to five – Five! But that's the only time I think I might not like five. Five of the same cartoon would be too much! Like when the little baby (like Tahbey used to be) goes home to its Daddy, why do the cartoon animals have to do other things after that? They did their work: tiger, fuzzy elephant, and ugly thing take the baby home – end of story. I don't want to see them do other things - that's stupid.

I like movies, even though Daddy only lets me watch one a night now, but baths? Baths are even better. Baths mean water!

I love water….

Chapter Five

Water is the greatest thing ever. You can do so many things with water! Water is better than numbers. Water is even better than five! Five! Water is great for playing in, for swimming in, for drinking, for splashing, for throwing rocks in, for dipping things in. I love water. I love it so much that I have to drink out of sippy-cups like Tahbey does at home. I can drink out of a regular cup everywhere else, but at home I get so into playing with the water in my cup that I end up making a mess. Milk, coffee, tea, juice, and pop are good too, but I get distracted with those just like water. I like to dip cookies into milk or coffee, and once I figured pizza was so good in dippy white stuff it might be good to try dipping it in Daddy's coffee. It wasn't so I left it in the mug … that was when Daddy said I had to go back to sippy-cups like Tahbey. But it was his coffee. He should have been drinking it if he didn't want me dipping food in it, right? Or he could have been using one of those adult sippy-cups they take with them in cars. If I couldn't touch the water or coffee or whatever, then I wouldn't dip things in it.

Baths and swimming pools are great! I can dip myself into the water! Just like a big piece of food into dippy white stuff. The water blocks the fog. If I hold my breath and dive under, the fog can't find me. I can hide for a few seconds. It's the only place

I've found that's safe from the fog. I wish I could hold my breath forever, or be like a fish, they can breathe even in the water. I learned about fish at the zoo with Daddy. Sometimes we go to the pool. I love the pool, but I don't like it so much when there are a bunch of other kids screaming and running around splashing. The pool, all that water, is the one place I can understand that word relax Daddy uses when he talks about music without words. So if other kids are at the pool acting like it's recess we leave. The fog leaves when the water hides me, but if I can't get in the water because of the other kids, the fog takes advantage of me being upset and pushes on me real hard.

That's why, even though I love the pool, baths are better. In a bath there's only me and the water. Sometimes Mommy gets worried because I hold my breath so long. She pops her head in the door and reaches into the water, shaking me. I can't hear her in the water, but when I sit up she's saying, "Megan, don't stay under so long. It scares me," or something like that.

I smile and play with some bubbles, but once she leaves to do something else, I slip right back under for as long as I can. I know when I have to come out to breathe, but if I lean way back and the water is high enough I can leave my mouth or nose out and still breathe while I'm under the water.

The Fog Within

I stay in as long as I can. I stay in my bath until the water goes from warm to cold. I don't know why it does that. I wish it would stay warm. When I was little, two, three, four, or five! Five! years old, Daddy used to turn the water back on to warm it up for me. But, like the movies, I'd start to want the water all the time. I'd jump out of the tub, run down the hall and eat a few bites of food, and then run all the way back down to the tub and jump back in. I'd stay in all day long, or I'd scream when Daddy wouldn't let me have a bath. Daddy said he wanted me to have fun, but it wasn't doing me any good if he spoiled me, so I only get to have one bath a day – unless I have an accident or I make a really big mess. What does that mean, spoiled? More stupid grown-up rules I think. If I want to be in the tub all day long then why not? The water comes out of that pipe in the wall. I know how to turn it on. I wish I could tell Daddy that the water hides me from the fog. I bet he'd let me stay in as long as I wanted to then … but, I think Daddy might know anyway. He helps me where he can, but I guess some things are just there like the fog. We can't hide from them no matter how scared they make us, or how much we might want them to go away.

Daddy doesn't have to tell me it's time for my bath to be over. When I start to get cold I climb out of the bathtub and jump up and down at the gate they put in the doorway so Tahbey doesn't climb in with me. Tahbey likes baths too. He sits in front of the gate most of the time I take a bath, hoping I'll help him over so he can get in with me. Or, since I'm distracted in the tub, he'll play with the toys I don't like him to have when I'm out like my computer. Tahbey can play a lot of the same games I can on my computer. He sits next to me and watches. Then when I'm busy he plays. It makes me mad that he can do the same things I can and he's so small. I don't think Tahbey has the fog bothering him, making it hard for him to see what's real. He's lucky.

Tahbey isn't playing with the computer when I finish my bath tonight. He stands up when I get out and yells, "Megan done! Megan done!"

Daddy comes around the corner from the kitchen wiping his hands on a towel. Tahbey is still yelling that I'm done, over and over. Daddy reaches down and while he opens the gate for me to get out of the bathroom, he says to Tahbey, "Thanks buddy, I can see that."

I run past Daddy into the living room, dropping my towel in the hallway on top of Tahbey's head. I like being naked, but Mommy and Daddy are always telling me to put clothes on. More stupid grown-up rules. Dogs and cats don't wear clothes. Raccoons and fish don't wear clothes. Daddy says, "Dude!" and he gives me a wide-eyed look and spreads his hands out. I laugh and run back into the bathroom to get my pajamas. I can put them on myself, but I figure if I want to be naked then I'm going to make

The Fog Within

Mommy or Daddy dress me. If they want the clothes on, then they can do it. Daddy helps me put my pajamas on while Tahbey still struggles to get out from under the wet towel.

Same thing goes for brushing my teeth. I make Daddy do it. If it's something I don't want to do, fog or no fog, then the grown-up who came up with the idea has to make me do it. Why should I help if I don't want to do it in the first place? That's stupid. That's something only a grown-up would do.

Tahbey escapes from the towel and climbs all over my bed and plays with my pillows while Daddy tries to get me ready for bed. It's funny to watch. Daddy picks Tahbey up and puts him on the floor, then shuts my windows, Tahbey climbs back up, Daddy puts him back down and he does something else. They go back and forth one, two, three times, before Daddy gives me a kiss and says, "Goodnight Megan. I love you sweetheart."

I kiss him back and sometimes if I remember, or if I'm not really tired and ready for bed, I give him a hug too. I forget some nights and then I'm mad at myself for forgetting. Daddy turns out the light, and takes a giggling Tahbey with him. I toss and turn under my covers for a while before I fall asleep. When I dream I have trouble telling what's real and what's dream. When I'm awake the fog distorts things so much that dreams and real life just blur most of the time – living with the fog is like living a dream you never wake up from.

I'm running in the woods. The trees are dropping their red, orange, and yellow leaves. Daddy's behind me and I'm laughing. I run some more to see how fast I can go, but when I turn around Daddy's gone. I run back the other way looking for him, even faster because I'm starting to get scared. But he's gone. I'm lost. The trees change. The leaves fall back up, clinging to the trees, and turn green. They choke the path so I can't see where I'm going. I'm really scared…

…Lost, where's Daddy? Help, Mommy? Tahbey? Trees everywhere, moving, rocking, creaking, laughing, yelling. The trees have faces. Scared. The trees have mouths. The trees are screaming, "Fear us! Fear us!" Lost in, green, red, orange, yellow, black. Can't see. Help! The trees!…

…I open my eyes and my room is still dark. I jump out of bed and turn on the light. I'm scared, but I'm back in my room. The fog is gone, but I can feel my heart pounding in my chest. I'm sweating. I leave the light on and pace my room for a while, shuffling my bare feet on the carpet to feel the rough texture on my feet. Rough and smooth, help me block the fog, help me slow my heart down. I don't like it when it beats so fast from being scared; beating fast from jumping is fun, but beating fast from scared hurts. I walk around my room for a long time. I look to the door hoping Mommy will come in and ask me to help her work. I don't remember if I fell back asleep or not.

Chapter Six

It was another hard morning. Daddy didn't have to drag me out of bed. I was awake and waiting for him to open the door. Daddy must have had a rough night too, because he didn't bother with a plate of food that I wouldn't eat. When I sat down at my usual spot there was a half a cup of coffee and five Oreo cookies. Five! I think Daddy sees through the fog sometimes. He was leaning against the counter drinking his own coffee and watching me. I was busy pulling my cookies apart, eating the soft white stuff, and then dunking the hard black cookies into my coffee. He says, "We're going to see a new therapist today after school, Megan."

Therapist! That's what the teacher not teachers are called. I always forget - grown-ups need names for everything. I've been to lots of teachers not teachers, I mean therapists. They all smile and are nice. They try to get me to play, or color, or work, or whatever they want to call it. Some of them try to get me to talk using my hands, or by using pictures, since the fog won't let them hear my voice. Usually I get upset waiting or they want me to do something grown-up and stupid, so I have less control over the fog. The fog is really hard to push back when I have to wait in one of those *Waiting Rooms*. The whole point of being in the room is to wait. Isn't that crazy? Who would come up with an idea like that? A room to wait in – sheesh. Even without the fog making me hear, see, or smell things that aren't there, a room for waiting would make me want to pull my hair out.

I don't let Daddy know that I heard him. He doesn't care. He knows I heard him, and he knows that I know that I heard him. He finished his coffee while he packed my lunch in my bag within bags and went to get my jacket and shoes. Just like with putting clothes on after my baths - baths have water, I love water! - when it's time for school Daddy has to put my jacket and shoes on for me, or I won't. I don't know why some days I go to school five days in a row. Five! And why others I have days off. Why not every day, or every other day? Why five days? Maybe the grown-ups who make the rules know how awesome five is too. Five! Maybe all their made up grown-up rules aren't so dumb if they understand five!

Dressed and in the car listening to music, I can feel the fog pushing on me – hard. The music isn't cutting it this morning. I growl a little bit. I don't know if I'm growling at the fog, Daddy, or the music, but it feels like I should growl, so I do. Daddy looks at me in that tiny face mirror. He says, "You alright, Megan?"

I growl and bounce up and down in my seat a few times. The good part about Daddy is that he'll treat that as if I said, "I don't know, Daddy. I'm just angry this morning."

He nods his head and says, "Alright, I feel you, just chill out a little bit please."

I stop bouncing, but keep growling, and he says, "That's my girl."

It feels like I'm at school and in my room without ever getting there. I don't remember Daddy walking me to the door and my teacher coming to get me. I don't remember the fog pushing in and scaring me either. I remember being in the car and growling and then I'm sitting at my desk. How did that happen? It happens a lot. The fog steals memories from me. I think that's mean and cruel. You should be able to remember the things you do, or why do them, right?

I look over at brown haired girl ... Sally? Yeah, Sally. She's rocking in her chair and boss teacher is telling the other teachers something. The other kids are watching a movie on the wall screen full of those Muppet things. I don't like Muppets. They creep me out. Are they supposed to be real? They talk to real people, so they aren't cartoons, but I've never seen a Muppet in person. If I did, and it wasn't the fog causing me to see it, I think I'd run away - creepy little things. Well, if nobody is looking at me, teachers are talking and the other kids are watching, so I'm getting a snack out of my bag within bags. I get up and walk over while the teachers keep on talking. I don't hear anybody say my name which means they aren't paying attention. They're too busy talking over all of us. If there is a movie playing on the wall most of my friends in the room will stare at it and sit still, or rock like Sally. They'll watch anything. They're nice kids but they don't know a good cartoon from a creepy Muppet. When everybody else is distracted, which happens all the time, I see it as a chance to do what I want. Right now, I want a cookie. In my bag I find that Daddy only packed me: one, two cookies. Only Two?

I could eat them both, but I look over and see Sally watching me. She smiles. I like Sally. She lets me run my fingers through her soft brown hair. I look over at the teachers. They're still talking over us. Good. Sally isn't supposed to have certain foods. All the teachers say Sally can only have certain things because if she eats cookies, or bread, or pizza - yeah I know pizza! - she'll act worse. How could food make her act worse? Food is fun. How could food make the fog worse for Sally? I don't think it's fair that Sally can't have pizza or cookies, unless they're made just for her. They call them Glue-free cookies or something. Who puts glue in food? I tried one of her cookies once. It tasted like butt – gross butt! If the teachers aren't looking I give Sally some of the foods I like, so I gave Sally my other cookie. She smiles and eats it real fast because she knows if the teachers see it they'll take it away. It's funny because I've been giving Sally all the stuff the grown-ups say she isn't supposed to have for a long time, and they still say things like, "Oh her behavior is improving with the diet." They talk over us and don't think we understand, but sometimes I can see through the fog. I can see that it isn't hurting Sally to eat what I do, so I go ahead with that sharing thing everybody always wants me to do.

Why should I share sometimes and not others? More stupid grown-up rules. I wonder if grown-ups follow their own rules or if they just yell at us kids and make us follow them instead.

Recess was bad today too. The fog had been pushing on me all morning, more than normal, really a lot since last night. Last night was scary. But on recess I kept pacing and running my hands against the bricks to feel that tingly touch. It helped with the fog. There was a group of other kids, both boys and girls, I don't know their names. I wonder if they have names. I thought they were happy at first because they were laughing. But not all laughing is because you are happy. There are other kinds of laughing. Some laughing is good – that's the laughing I do – but there are mean kinds of laughing, too. They were doing the other kind of laugh, the laughing that isn't laughing. Their mouths move and they make the noise a laugh makes, but their eyes are mean and angry like they want to hurt you. Their eyes give them away. I don't like looking in their eyes. They look like the eyes on the faces of the trees in my bad dream. They were laughing the mean laugh and when I'd walk past them a few would say,

The Fog Within

"Megan Cooper, Megan Cooper." I thought, Yes, that's my name. So I'd look up, but then they'd say, "Is dumber than a pooper scooper!" and then laugh that mean laugh.

I just wanted the fog to leave me alone for a few minutes. Recess isn't fun as it is, so all I wanted was to touch the brick wall and feel the tingles in my fingers. I wanted to feel something that wasn't there - something that I *knew* wasn't there, and I had control over - but they wouldn't leave me alone. They stood at the corner where the teachers couldn't see them. I knew I could have shortened my walk. I could have walked in a smaller section near the teachers and they wouldn't be laughing the mean laugh … but, the fog, you see the fog won't let me do that. I have to walk the entire length of the wall before I can turn around. I want to turn around halfway so I don't have to hear them laughing, but I can't. The fog won't let me do what I want to, so I try to stop listening to their mean laughter. Most times I can trick myself into thinking the mean laughter is the other kind of laughing, or it could be the fog. It could always be the fog. Maybe the kids weren't being mean to me. I don't know what a pooper scooper is? Is it a joke? I play jokes with Daddy. We hide from Tahbey and jump out and say, "Boo!" Maybe it's like that.

I don't know. I never do. I can't trust the fog and I can't trust other kids either. I'd like for them to just let me play with their hair like Sally does if they're a girl. That would be nice. I don't know what the boys do; maybe jump on a trampoline like I do with Daddy. Trampolines are fun!

I was really happy when it was time for recess to be over, so I could go in and have lunch. I was happy while I walked with my teacher to the lunchroom and she picked out my food for me. Macaroni and cheese, okay, not great, but okay. Daddy makes it better than school does. I was still happy when I walked over and threw the parts I didn't want away. When we were walking back to my classroom the fog swept in fast and hard. I don't know what caused it. I thought touching the bricks at recess had been enough, but one minute I was walking, the next...

...Anger, anger, mad, red, sad. Faces, laughing... not laughing. Eyes mean, eyes angry, eyes hate, eyes on fire, eyes, eyes, eyes. Yelling, who's yelling? Me? Is it Megan yelling? No, teacher? Yes, no, not yelling, teacher scared. Megan scared! Eyes! Laughing! Hate!...

...I remember being back in the car with Daddy. How did I get there? What happened after the fog pulled me away from school? I was in the hall and then after the fog left me my next memory was of being in the backseat, looking at the back of Daddy's head. The music was playing, nice music with mumbled words. Tahbey didn't come with Daddy today. Daddy looks at me in the small black mirror and says, "You alright, MC?"

I use my fingers to tell Daddy I'm thirsty. He says, "Sure thing," and hands me back a sippy-cup. I look out the window. We aren't driving home. This isn't the way home. I know the way home. I ride it all the time. I also know the way to the pizza store, the taco place, the pool, the zoo, and my grandparents' house. We aren't driving anywhere near those places. More buildings pass by, the houses look like faces. Sad faces. The windows look like eyes. I'm tired. The fog waking me up two nights in a row is making me tired. When I'm tired I don't focus as well ... the world sort of drifts by, floating, kind of there but not there. I don't know if Daddy likes to talk to himself (because he does that a lot) or, if he's trying to be nice and talk to me like another grown-up – to me, not over me. I can hear him talking away as he drives like he would to another adult. It's like he's talking over me, because I don't understand most of it, but he's still trying to talk to me.

"I tell you, Megan. I wish we didn't have to keep going to new therapists and doctors and neurologists and on and on, man oh man. I'm a people person, but I get tired of explaining all your idiosyncrasies to new people. It wears me out. I know you hate it, kiddo, and I hate it too. I wish I could just let you have my damn voice. I don't need it. Nobody listens to me anyway. I wish I could help."

I wish he could too. I wouldn't take Daddy's voice. I don't even know what he means, but I wish he could push the fog away for me. So I could tell him I love him instead of just giving him a kiss. Daddy has yelled at me plenty of times, not as much as Mommy, but he still has. But Daddy has never done that laughing not laughing at me. He has never looked at me with those not happy eyes. He looks at me with sad eyes sometimes and tired eyes, but not eyes that want to hurt me. Eyes are weird. White circles with colored circles with black dots. Eyes are circles with a lot of things in them – eyes are scary.

I lose track of where we are again - different buildings that look like different faces. I don't know why the fog is taking chunks of my day from me today. It does that sometimes when it's really bad, other times I can remember the whole day – start to finish ... but not today. There are other days that I remember. Those days may not even be real. They may be fog days. Memories all created by the fog and not stuff that I really lived through. Those are sad days. Sad and tired days like Daddy's eyes. Daddy stops the car in a parking lot and gets out. When he opens my door he says, "Come on, Megan. Let's go meet your new therapist."

Chapter Seven

Of course when we walked in the door there was a waiting room. Why? Why? Why? Always, every time I have to go somewhere for a doctor or therapist there is a waiting room. Waiting sucks! I hate waiting! If these people are supposed to help me with the fog don't you think they'd know how much waiting sucks gross butt? If they do, they don't seem to realize it, or like most grown-ups, they don't care about the fog. They just follow their rules like stupid ticking clock hands and never wonder why a room for waiting would cause a person with the fog so much agitation.

We didn't have to use the waiting room though. A woman with yellow brown hair was waiting in the room for us. She was waiting for us! That was a nice change. She smiled at Daddy and held her hand out for him to shake. They talked over me for a minute until I started to growl because they were making me wait. The woman leaned down to look at me and says, "Hi Megan! I'm Jessie. Do you want to come play with me?" and she holds her hand out for me to take. She talks to me in that happy grown-up voice that is too happy. Nobody is that happy. But I smile back because she's smiling and her eyes aren't mean, hurtful eyes; they're happy eyes.

I take her hand and she leads me down a hallway. Daddy stays in the waiting room. Daddy's weird. He lays down over three chairs and tilts his hat over his eyes like he's pretending to sleep. But I can see under the hat and he's watching everybody and everything as we walk away. I know this lady, this therapist says, "Play," but she means work, or some other weird thing she'll try to get me to do. But, that's still better than the waiting room. I don't need Daddy to come with me, but if I were him I'd have come just to avoid the waiting room, pretending to sleep or not. The therapist not teacher leads me down another hall and then opens a door to a room. The room is small. My bedroom is bigger. She says, "This is my office, Megan. This is where I play, do you want to play?"

Sure lady, I'll play just give me a computer so I can play that game where I flick the colored bird heads at the green pig heads, or something like that, but I know she doesn't mean that kind of play. She wants me to play therapy games. Stuff that works on some of those big words therapists, doctors, and teachers are always saying around me like that manual dexti-thingy. She turns and shuts the door and I growl. The fog doesn't like when I'm shut in a room, unless I'm the one who shuts the door. The lady says, "Oh darn! That's right your father said something about that," and she opens the door again. She looks at me and asks, "Megan, would you shut the door for me?"

The Fog Within

I shut it, but I slam it. Not because the fog wanted me to, but because it made a really loud sound. Loud sounds can be fun ... but only if I make them. Plus if she knew about my door rule then she should have remembered up front, so I felt a slam was in order. The therapist doesn't react to the noise though and she says, "Okay Megan, thank you. Now would you like to play on the computer with me?"

I bump my fist along my arm a couple of times like Daddy showed me for a sign for computer. Not everybody gets my signs. Daddy says, "She gets the idea, but she does it half-assed, or her own way. Think of it like a New Yorker talking to someone from the Deep South. They can both say the same thing but it sounds different, and they only have the vaguest clue what the other person said."

I don't know what half of my ass - that means butt! - has to do with my signs but Daddy's said it enough times that the fog lets me remember. If I hear something enough times, I'll remember it, like when I thought autism was part of my name because I heard it so much. The yellow brown haired therapist understood my sign though and she says, "Very good, Megan! Yes computer." She repeated the motion I did only she held her hand differently – whatever, I was close enough, sheesh.

She pulls out a touchscreen computer. My favorite! I like any kind of anything with a screen: TVs, computers, phones, but I like the touch computers best. I can move through pages and drag things into place a lot easier. Touch computers are easy. I like easy. I take the computer from the lady's hands and sit down on her wheelie-chair. I like wheelie-chairs too because you can spin on them – real fast! I don't spin though. I flip through her computer looking for good games. She doesn't have any of the ones I like. No colored bird heads or that red Muppet guy with the big eyes that's always laughing like he's being tickled. Tahbey likes the red Muppet ... but you know how I feel about creepy Muppets. They have some good touch computer games though. I'll tolerate Muppets if it's a good game. But without any good games on her computer I start looking for better games. I have the different push button things - Daddy calls them menus but I thought that's what they give you to pick your food from at those places where you eat - open and I'm looking for good games when the therapist says, "Whoa, Megan, hold-on I thought I had that locked out."

I like to flip through and dig up different games on touch computers. It's really easy and I know how to use them better than most grown-ups. The therapist is flipping her fingers through the computer pages and talking quietly to herself like Daddy does sometimes. "How the hell did she do that? I didn't even know that was an option. Was it under 'Settings'? Where the..."

59

The Fog Within

She keeps going like that so I start to look around her room. She has all kinds of things that look like they might be fun to touch, but she'd probably yell at me if I did. Not *yell*, yell, but that stupid grown-up trying to be calm but can't voice, and say something like. "No Megan, that's not a choice."

Teachers and therapists love to give me choices: one, two, or three choices. Never five. Five! Because that would be nice, but, five choices are too many. They never let me have five choices. The therapist lady is still talking to herself, trying to figure out what I did to her computer, so I start to walk around the room. She looks up and says, "Megan honey, stay in the room please."

Please, what kind of word is that? I used to make the hand sign for please when I wanted something, but hand signs are a lot of work and I like easy, so I figured out if I just gave Daddy a kiss instead of the sign for please, he'd give me what I wanted. It's easier and it makes Daddy happy. I think people would be happier if you kissed them more and said please less.

I'm about to start touching stuff because I'm getting bored in the therapist's office, then I see something on her desk that bothers me. A spoon. It's just sitting there by the typing thing on her other computer, but I don't like it. I hate spoons! I'm not sure what to do. This isn't school, but it isn't home either. It isn't a place to eat with menus, so maybe the spoon isn't supposed to be there. I start to growl. The therapist says, "In a second, Megan."

No, that spoon shouldn't be there. It has no business in this room. I grab the spoon, run over to the door, and open it. The therapist lady says, "Megan honey, wait!"

But I don't care. I have to get rid of the spoon. I run down the hallway. I can't remember which way goes to the waiting room with Daddy and the door to leave. The spoon needs to go and I can hear the therapist catching up to me. I yank open the nearest door and throw the spoon into that room. I slam the door and walk back toward the therapist. She's breathing like Daddy does when he chases Tahbey and me around the house. She says, "Megan, what's wrong? What was that all about?"

Another woman comes out of the door that I threw the spoon into and says one of those bad words, then starts talking to the therapist over me. They're talking fast and loud. Real fast like Mommy does sometimes when she's mad at Daddy.

Daddy! I see Daddy walking down the hallway where the two ladies are talking really fast over me. He smiles at me. I smile back. Daddy interrupts the two fast talking ladies and says, "Let me guess, a spoon?"

They all start to talk over me. Daddy reaches out and ruffles my hair, then starts to tickle my neck when he hears me growling because we're now waiting, not playing, or working, or whatever it is we were supposed to be doing. Tickling distracts me sometimes and other times it makes me mad that Daddy is trying to distract me. I don't want to be distracted. I growl louder, but they don't stop. Daddy says, "I know, MC. Hold on a little longer I need to tell Jessie about some more things I forgot like spoons. So this…"

…Wait, wait, wait, hate wait! Pull hair, ouch! Ouch! Feel pain instead of wait! Pain better than wait. Stop, go, start, red, ouch! No faces! Just eyes! Go away eyes! Pain, pull, shove, yank…

…Daddy's driving the car again. He looks up at me from the little black mirror and says, "You make one hell of a first impression, MC." But he isn't mad. He's smiling and laughing so I smile and laugh back. He goes back to watching the road. I say, "Dat!" So he'll look back up at me, and I make the sign with my fist for coffee. Daddy laughs harder and says, "What the fuck! Why not? It's not like a little caffeine could cause that bald spot you just pulled out of your hair. I'd like to hear a doctor blame *that* on coffee."

He's talking to himself I know. That's just Daddy, but he says, "You deserve it anyway, Megan.

What was she thinking, a spoon in her office. You took care of that, didn't you?"

He's laughing that laugh of his. It's not a mean laugh, not a laugh like the kids at school. No it's like he's so tired that everything is funny. It's a sad laugh. I don't want Daddy to sad laugh because of me, so I better remember to give him a kiss when he stops and goes into a store to get us a coffee to share. That will help him stop the sad laugh … I … I hope I remember.

Chapter Eight

The next day was not a school day. I only know this because I'm awake early and Daddy doesn't come get me. The sun is up and I'm still stuck in my room waiting for Daddy. Waiting isn't so bad in my room. Sometimes it can be, but Mommy and Daddy always leave most of my favorite books and stuff in my room at night, because they know the fog wakes me up. I even have my own music headphones that I can listen to. It was bad when I was real little - as young as Tahbey little. I used to run around all night. I'd sleep for an hour or two then be up for an hour or two, and fall back asleep for an hour or two, and back and forth. The fog was real bad back then. It used to tell me to chew on things, anything: rocks, sticks, stones, the windowsills in my room, my bed rails, and the doorframe. Daddy says I even ate some nasty things he won't tell me about. I don't really remember eating the things the fog wanted me to. The further I look back the thicker the fog is. I can't see too far into my past. It's just one big blur of fog and emotions before about the time Daddy says I was three.

Not this morning. I'm up. I'm up, up, up and awake. No fog pushing or pulling at me. I look out the window and see sun and green grass and – then I hear the sound I've been waiting for, it's a click. Daddy unlocked my door. I sprint out the door and knock Tahbey down as I race past him in the hall. He says, "Megan!" But I run past. I have to pee. Mommy and Daddy put me in what they call special underwear at night, but it's a diaper. I don't want to wear a diaper, even at night. I'm a big kid. I'm not a baby like Tahbey. Daddy says it's okay to use the special underwear, but I don't want to. I know he has to lock my door because of the fog. If it wakes me up and I don't have control I might leave the house and not realize it, or go into Tahbey's room and wake him up. Once, before Tahbey started to live with us, the fog woke me up and I opened my door. The gate they use to keep Tahbey out of the bathroom was in front of my bedroom doorway. I looked at it and realized I could lift the middle bar and the gate would open. It was easy. I went into the living room to find something to do. There wasn't anything and I got bored, so I ran into Daddy's room and jumped on him. He yelled. He said some of those bad words and, "Megan, it's three a.m. What the hell?"

Three isn't as good as five, Five! I wonder if I'd woken him up at five if it would have been okay … probably not. It doesn't matter because after that time Daddy started to lock my door at night. I know it's because of the fog, but still, maybe I wouldn't be locked in if I hadn't jumped so hard on him. He gets grumpy when he's tired, or sad.

Today I don't want to use my special underwear and I've been holding it since I woke up. I don't know what number I woke up at, but it was still dark outside. I make it to the toilet, but it's a close thing. Tahbey's still yelling at me from the hallway. I hear Daddy say, "What buddy?"

"Megan pushed," Tahbey says.

"Well she probably had to pee," Daddy says. "Get out of her way next time. We go through this every morning little man."

"Megan push!" Tahbey yells as I finish up and walk out of the bathroom. I walk past him and tap him on the head. He yells, "Hey!" but gets up and follows me into the kitchen. Mommy must be in bed already because their bedroom door is shut and Daddy is trying to get some food ready. It isn't ready so I yell, "Dat!" to let him know I'm hungry. This isn't early like a school day. This is later and I'm hungry now. Tahbey climbs up into a seat next to me and yells, "Dat!" louder than I did, so I yell, "Dat!" again even louder. Tahbey yells it, then I yell it, then Tahbey yells it, then I yell it, then Daddy says another bad word and tosses a couple of food pocket things onto the table in front of us. I tear mine open down the middle and eat the cheese and meat out first, then if I'm still hungry and I can't get Daddy to give me another one, I'll eat the crust. Tahbey picks his up and eats like Daddy. Tahbey does what the grown-ups do. Unless it's something fun like yelling at Daddy, then he'll do things my way. It's fun to play jokes on Daddy, maybe that's all the mean-eyed kids at school are doing, playing jokes like Tahbey and I do, and they just aren't as happy about it.

After I eat I start asking Daddy for stuff: computer, more food, books, more food, my computer again, then I drag him down the hall to tickle and wrestle on my bed. It's a good morning, even having to dodge Tahbey when he tries to play with us. Since it isn't a school day, after lunch Daddy says, "Who wants to go to the zoo?"

Tahbey yells, "Zoo! Zoo!" and I try to say yes. It comes out all garbled and not what I meant to say. Sometimes I can say, "Yeah" real easy to a question and other times the fog changes the sounds. But I jump up and down and go get my shoes and jacket. I think dressing myself is enough of a yes for Daddy because he starts getting his bag ready. It's a bag like Mommy has, but it has more stuff in it, not just makeup and gum. Daddy's bag has diapers for Tahbey, juice for all of us, extra clothes, wipes, food, candy, and other stuff. Whenever we go someplace for longer than a few minutes Daddy takes his bag. I used to throw up a lot. I think Daddy still thinks I will, so he brings extra stuff in case I do: clean clothes for me, wipes, rags, and plastic bags to put dirty clothes in. I ate a whole bag of chocolate chips once and threw up all over the back of the car. It was gross. Mommy yelled, Daddy started to yell, but then they both laughed that tired sad laugh, which is better than yelling, I guess. So even though I don't eat whole bags of chocolate chips anymore, Daddy still packs his bag as if I do.

I love the zoo. We live a short drive from it. I can listen to more than five - Five! - songs in the car during the drive. So it's further than school but not too far. Daddy takes us there a lot because he knows how much we both like animals. When we go he parks and puts Tahbey in his stroller before he opens my door. Tahbey is squirming and trying to get down. He says, "No, no ride. Walk, walk zoo!"

Daddy says, "Tough shit, I have to watch both you and Megan and you're easier to strap down, buddy. You're riding."

I don't know why shit would be tough (is that when it hurts to go?), or what it has to do with Tahbey riding in the stroller, but it means I can go through the zoo my way and not have to wait for Tahbey to catch up, so I'm happy. I stop to look at the animals, but once I see the lion do I need to stare at it like Tahbey? It's a lion, yes, I see it, now onto the next animal. The only place I pause for longer and stare like Tahbey does is at the giant fish tank. It's amazing! All that water! I think it would be wonderful to be one of those colorful fish, floating, swimming, and swaying through the water all day long. I'll stay at the giant fish tank until Tahbey starts whining to move on.

I like to go around the zoo as many times as Daddy will let me. I'm hoping one day he'll let me go around five – Five! – times. But the most we've done so far is three. Daddy says, "Megan, I'm tired. Todd wants to play at the playground, or stretch his legs, or something." So, we stop and play on one of the zoo playgrounds. I know I could do two more laps to make five – Five! – while Daddy plays with Tahbey, but Daddy won't let me do it on my own, so he gives me a cookie and hands me my headphones so I can listen to music while Tahbey plays. I used to play on playgrounds, but when the other parents started looking at me weird I stopped. A lot of other kids' parents act like I might give their kid the fog too. That just by me being around their kid and doing something they think is weird, I'll rub off on them. Some of these moms put sweaters on their dogs and they think I'm weird? It's a dog, it has fur.

We don't go for another two laps. Daddy says we have to get back home. It's time for Mommy to wake up and Tahbey needs a nap. Awake, asleep, awake, asleep. Who says they need to be awake or asleep. Tahbey doesn't want a nap and when we get home and Mommy comes out of the bedroom she looks like she should have squeezed herself under her mattress and slept longer. Nobody asks me what I think about these stupid rules. Daddy would probably listen … if I could tell him.

Chapter Nine

I had one more not school day and then it was right back. Sometimes there are longer breaks between school days. I like the longer breaks. Sometimes the days I don't go are so many in a row that I forget that I have to go back. Those long breaks are because of the colored lights, trees, and gifts, and other times it's because of the heat, I think. The days I don't go because of the heat are the longest break. I can sleep when I want, but I get bored easy too. School would be more fun if there were less rules. I'd rather go and have fun ... go and do something other than sit around the house all day. Daddy tries to play games with me, but Tahbey and I don't always like to do the same things. School gives me something to do without dragging Tahbey along. I like painting and playing with my brown haired friend ... Sally? Sally! I just don't like how the fog makes everything harder for me than the other kids without it. Even for the other kids in my class. Some of them kind of have the fog bothering them. I can tell because they don't always seem to know what's going on, they look scared, but most of the others have problems walking and moving and stuff like that.

I don't know which is worse. I can move, run, skip, dance, and all kinds of other things, but the fog makes it so I miss out on so much. I know there are things going on around me that I'm supposed to enjoy during the school breaks. Things with lights, trees, cakes, and when people come over, but I don't get that. Why does that happen sometimes and not others? If I could trade the fog for not being able to run or skip, I think I would. I'd miss running. I bet the boy with the metal boots in my class would like to run, but he doesn't have the fog screaming and pressing at him all the time. He even doesn't mind using spoons. Spoons! Can you believe that? I bet it's nice to not have the fog rip away pieces of your day. I hate the fog.

The first day of my five – Five! days of school wasn't too bad. It was there and then gone like a lot of my days. It was the second day that was bad. It blurred into the other three with too much fog. I know I've said it's hard to tell when some of the other kids are laughing that mean laugh or if they're laughing with me. It is. I can't always look them in the eye, and if I do sometimes the fog changes what's there so I don't know if it's good or bad. It could be the fog – real, but not real.

The second day of school that week I had an accident at recess. That doesn't happen very often. I know how to use a toilet. I'm not stupid, but … sometimes if the fog is pushing on me hard, distracting me, it can be a mad dash because by the time I realize I need to go – I need to GO! So, on recess as I was running my fingers along the bricks and enjoying the tingle, I realized I had to pee. I ran over to the teacher that was out watching us as she talked to another teacher. I grabbed her hand and she said, "What Megan? It isn't time for lunch yet."

I growled. I knew it wasn't time for lunch. I wasn't even hungry. I had to pee!

"You'll just have to wait to eat, Megan. We go through this every day," she said and continued to talk over me to the other teacher. I pulled on her hand but she pulled it away and ignored me, so I ran back toward the building. I got through the doors and I heard one of the teachers calling after me. Almost, I almost made it to the bathroom, but I lost control halfway down the hall, just as another class was getting out to go to recess. I hate how pee goes from hot to cold so fast. I was cold and wet. I heard one of the other kids yell, "Megan peed her pants! Megan peed her pants!" Other kids started yelling or laughing what I'm pretty sure was the mean laugh. I was scared and embarrassed. Not a good way to keep the fog from sweeping over me. I don't remember the teacher getting to me. The last thing I remember is one girl screaming, "Eww gross! What's wrong with her?" and then the fog was there…

…Mad, scared, sad! Go away! Go away! Help me! Somebody help me! Daddy please, I want Daddy! Faces, mean faces and angry eyes! Cold, so cold, please help. Go away! Blue, blue, cold, wet,

smells of soap and dust. Help! Who's there? Anybody please? Help me! Go away!...

...I was back in my classroom. I don't know if I ate lunch or not. I don't remember. The teachers were showing us something up on the big wall computer. I didn't care. I didn't want to watch. The fog was gone, for now, it never goes away completely. I was tired and my head hurt. I must have hurt myself while the fog pushed in on me. If I smack my head against something hard while the fog has ahold of me, hard enough to leave a welt and bruise, sometimes that helps the fog go away ... but sometimes it's the fog telling me to do it. I don't know if that's good or bad.

When it was time to go home I had to carry my pee-soaked jeans and underwear out to Daddy's car in a plastic bag. Daddy doesn't say anything. He just takes the plastic bag from me, along with my regular bag within bags, and helps me get in the car. Daddy doesn't yell when I have an accident, well sometimes if it's a big one at home he will. You know, of the other kind. He might yell, "Dude! Really?" But he doesn't scream and yell like the teachers do and sometimes Mommy yells about it too. And sometimes she doesn't. I don't know why sometimes it bothers her and other times it's okay. Maybe that's just the fog messing with me. I don't know.

The Fog Within

Tahbey wasn't with Daddy, so I didn't have him jabbering at me. Sometimes it bothers me that Tahbey can say more than I can and he doesn't even know to use the toilet yet! But I guess neither do I, stupid Megan! Stupid...

...Hurt, pull, hurt, yell! Scream!...

... "Whoa MC! Hold on there!" Daddy yells, reaching back from the front seat and squeezing my foot. "Chill out kiddo. I know you had a bad day, but just give me a few minutes and we'll be home. You can freak out on me all you want, but just wait until we aren't riding in a ton of plastic and steel doing 65 on the highway, okay?"

I didn't hear more than wait until we get home and between that and the pressure he's putting on my foot help me push the fog back a little. I don't remember much of that night, and the rest of the week was even worse. The kids at school kept laughing the mean-eyed laugh at me in the hallway if there wasn't a teacher around, or on the playground. By the end of the week I wanted to hide in my bedroom and be left alone ... but I still had to go see my new teacher not teacher, therapist lady again. I hope she doesn't have any spoons in her office this time.

Chapter Ten

The therapist not teacher was waiting for Daddy and me again in the waiting room. That really was a nice change. It would be nice if all doctors and therapist people had to wait in the room for me instead of the other way around. That would make more sense. They should be the ones waiting, not me. It's their office, not mine. So, they should wait, not me, right? If they came over to our house to see me I wouldn't make them wait in the living room forever until they could come down to my room to see me.

The therapist smiled and she leaned down, speaking in that extra-happy grown-up voice, "Hi Megan! Remember me, Jessie? Do you want to try playing with me again today?"

She asks like I have a choice. If I could say no I bet I'd still have to. I sigh and look over at the other people waiting. A lot of the people waiting look like my friends at school. I can tell there is something different about them, some have the fog and others have problems with their arms or legs or heads. I don't think it's fair to make people who already have problems wait for help. Jessie takes my hand and says, "I have my computer all set up for you and I double-checked my office for spoons," she says that part looking at Daddy. "Did I forget anything?"

The Fog Within

Daddy laughs and says, "No, but if you're going to play some music, I'd recommend the Boss or Bon Jovi. She doesn't like classical."

"Okay, I'll keep that in mind," she says as I start to growl because they are taking too long to talk. When we walk down to her smaller than my bedroom office, I notice that there are a lot less things sitting out. It's like Mommy came in and had one of her cleaning fits – everything is put away and there isn't much sitting out to distract me or for anybody to have much fun with. I wonder what she plays with in here when she's by herself. Therapist … Jessie? Yeah I think it was Jessie, sits down in her twirling, spinning chair and pulls another chair over next to her and says, "You can close the door if you want, Megan. Either way when you're done I'd like to show you my new games."

I thought about slamming the door. I like slamming doors just like I did last time I was there. It would be fun, but I was interested to see if she had added better games to her touch computer, which she had out on her desk. I left the door open and sat in the chair next to her. The screen on the computer looked like water. Water!

I ran my hands over it to test and see if the fog was playing tricks with my eyes, but it was still a touch computer. It wasn't real water and it wasn't the fog. Everywhere my fingers traced the computer water reacted like real water. The only difference was that I didn't actually get wet. It was like watching the giant fish tank at the zoo only there wasn't any fish in it. But unlike the fish tank I could make the water react to my touch. The fish tank is just cold glass. This was water, but not wet water. Jessie leaned over and brought the touch computer back to the menu. She says, "See, Megan, isn't that neat?"

I growl a little because I want the water not water back. Then she brings up another game with pictures. Oh boy, I know this one. Sure enough she pulls up a picture of water, taps it and the computer says, "Water." Nice, thanks, rub it in that the computer doesn't have the fog and it can talk but I can't – sheesh. Jessie says, "See, 'Water'. Anytime you want us to go back to the water instead of getting upset just press this button to ask."

I press the water button. She says, "Okay," and she turns it back to the water. I play with it for a while longer, tracing my fingers in the water not water. I can almost feel the water like touching a puddle. But then she goes back to the menu and brings up another picture. It's of a radio. She says, "How about some music? Do you want me to turn on some music, Megan?"

I touch the water button.

She says, "Okay fine," and she turns it back to the water screen. After a while of playing she goes back to the picture menu. I growl, but she ignores

77

me. She touches a picture of a cookie and says, "How about a cookie, Megan? Would you like a cookie?"

I would like a cookie. A cookie sounds really good and some coffee, but I'm not a dog looking for a treat, so I touch the water button. She sighs and asks, "Really Megan? Wouldn't you like to try something else?"

I touch the water button and growl and grind my teeth, so she knows I'm serious. She says, "Fine, but this is the last time. We need to try different things, Megan. It's good to try different things. That's how we learn."

All I heard was the word fine, but she kept on talking like Daddy does. I play with the water screen. It's nice. It's not as good as going to the pool, but it's still nice. When Jessie goes back to the picture menu I growl. She says, "I'm sorry Megan, but you need to try other things."

I growl and grind my teeth and start bouncing up and down in the chair so she knows I'm mad. My last resort is to wring my fingers and pound my head on her desk. I don't want to do that, but if I get mad enough and she doesn't realize I'm mad, those are the only things the fog will let me do. But she doesn't get upset with me. She doesn't get annoyed or angry that I'm not doing what she wants. She doesn't show me some silly card. I went to a school where if you did something wrong the teacher would show you a red card, or a green card if you did something good. It didn't matter if the red card was because the fog made you do it … or, if you did it not because of the fog, but just because you wanted to do it even though you knew it was wrong. I do things like that sometimes. I know a lot of people do. It's the closest I come to doing things like people without the fog when I do something I know I'm not supposed to, but I do it anyway. At that school the teacher would show me a tiny red card with a frowning face on it and say, "Megan, what you did made me sad, Megan. Red, sad!" I'd think red isn't sad. Red is mad. Blue is sad. I like colors. They are pretty and fun to touch and tickle. But if you're sad everybody says you're blue, right? Stupid grown-up rules and tiny red cards, even I know sad is blue, not red.

Jessie didn't show me a silly card or get upset that I was upset. She flipped through the picture menu until she found a cartoon of a mad face. She says, "Megan, are you mad?"

I growl. Yes I'm mad. What else do you want lady? She takes my hand and makes me touch the mad face. The computer that talks says, "Mad."

Jessie then pulled up a picture of me. Daddy must have given her one, and she says, "Megan – that's you." She makes me touch the Megan button and the computer says, "Megan."

79

The Fog Within

I'm still growling and grinding my teeth the whole time. I don't like being forced to do things. The fog is pushing really hard now that I'm mad and I'm about to start pulling on my hair or banging my head on her desk. I can feel it coming. Jessie has me touch the Megan button again and then the mad button. The computer says, "Megan mad."

I yank my hand away from therapist Jessie because I can feel the fog getting ready to sweep over me. But right before I lose myself in the fog, what the touch picture computer game said reached past the fog. Yes, I was mad. Megan mad. So I touched the Megan and mad buttons over and over really fast. The computer says, "Megan mad, Megan mad, Megan mad," over and over like Tahbey complaining about something.

Jessie isn't upset. She smiles and claps her hands as she says, "That's great, Megan! Now I know you're mad. So how can I help you not be mad?"

I sigh and growl at her. Then I touch the water button.

Jessie sighs too, but says, "Well it's a start."

Chapter Eleven

Daddy takes us all shopping the next day. It's a not school day so it's been an easy morning. I like to go shopping but most times Daddy does it when I'm at school. He says it's easier for him because he's already out from dropping me off at school, but I know it's easier for him to go without me so he doesn't have to worry about the fog. I understand, but wish he'd take me more often. I miss out on so much as it is with the fog. I hate that the fog takes things away from me that way too. Because even Daddy gets tired of dealing with it - Daddy and his sad tired eyes. Mommy is awake and we all go to the store together. I like to push the cart. Sometimes if Daddy isn't looking I push the cart (with Tahbey in it) into a corner and leave it there while Tahbey yells, "Hey!" It's funny, but Mommy's with us today so there is no way I'll be able to not have at least one of them watching me at all times. So I push the cart like I'm supposed to while Mommy and Daddy pick out food. Sometimes I add the stuff I want to the cart and sometimes Mommy takes it back out. I usually get most of the stuff I want though. If I put in more than Mommy takes out I'm happy.

Pushing Tahbey down the cereal box aisle an old lady I don't know stops Mommy and starts talking. I know they're talking about me, but over me. I'm not really trying to listen because I'm looking at all the cartoons on the boxes. I love cartoons, but I can never figure out what they have to do with the colored rings, balls, and marshmallows Daddy calls cereal. The old lady says, "Aw God bless her. What a big helper."

What does that mean? People say it around me all the time. They say, "God bless her," and I think - What, I didn't sneeze? Because that's what people say when you sneeze, right? God bless you. So did I sneeze and the fog made me not realize it? Are those people calling me a sneeze or a booger or something like that? I don't understand, but they keep saying it and it doesn't upset Mommy so it must be okay.

I don't like waiting in the checkout line when we're done shopping – no matter the store. I usually get to pick out a piece of candy, but it's hard to decide. One minute the checkout roller thing is full and the next Daddy says, "Come on, Megan. You have to pick something. You're holding up the line." So I grab a candy bar that the wrapper looks neat and pretty, but ends up tasting like butt. Tahbey will eat it though, so if it's butt candy I just give it to him. I wish I could remember which candy tastes like butt before we leave.

When we get home and Mommy and Daddy put all the food away, Daddy says, "Who wants to go to the pool?" because it's a not school day and we have more time to do fun things.

Tahbey runs around squealing at the idea of going to the pool. I jump up and down, giggling and laughing. We both love the pool – more than the zoo! Tahbey runs to get his shoes and trips and falls, banging his head on a chair. He cries. I run around him to get my shoes. Mommy picks up Tahbey and asks if he's okay, but Tahbey keeps crying. Daddy says, "Well that's too bad. I guess Todd will just have to stay here while Megan and I go to the pool."

Tahbey stops crying and wiggles to get down from Mommy's arms so he can get his shoes. He walks to get them that time, no happy squealing or sad crying. I'm ready, Tahbey's ready, Daddy's ready, Mommy's ready, and…

…No, not now! Want to swim! Eyes, faces, scared. Not now! Leave me alone. Eyes bugged out, scream! Pain, go away, help me. No, close eyes. No eyes! No…

… I fight the fog. I don't remember getting into the car or the drive there, but when I push the fog back as far as it will go Daddy's parking the car at the pool. I'm glad because sometimes if the fog pushes me away like that Daddy won't do what we were supposed to, or we leave what we were doing early. I think that isn't fair. The fog will go away for a bit and we could still go or stay, but the fog bothers Daddy and Mommy too much sometimes and we don't do anything because they're worried about what the fog will make me do in front of other people. It's not fair. Who cares what other people think of the fog? They don't have to live with it, so why should they care?

For a not school day the pool is pretty empty. There are only a few other kids splashing and swimming when we come out of the bathroom, locker room, smell like pee room, with our swimsuits on. Mommy takes Tahbey into the kiddie pool, but Daddy lets me swim in the grown-up pool. I like to jump off the side into the water and swim around under the surface with my eyes open like a fish. There's no fog underwater. The fog can't reach me until I surface. For a short time I'm safe and fog-free. Then I know I need to breathe so I push toward the surface and grab ahold of Daddy so I can catch my breath. Once I calm my breathing to normal, I jump off of Daddy and do the whole thing over again. In the water I'm not Megan. Under the water there's no me, no fog, no anything but the water.

I laugh the whole time because it's so much fun. I'm giggling and don't realize somebody has been talking to me other than Daddy. With all the splashing and diving it's hard to hear at the pool. I thought the voice talking to me was the fog at first so I dove back underwater, but when I had to come up to breathe there was a woman swimming next to Daddy. She looks familiar, but I don't realize who she is until she says, "Hi Megan. It's Jessie. Are you having fun swimming?"

Oh it's the therapist lady. I didn't recognize her here and not at her office. I have trouble with that sort of thing. If I don't see the person in the place that I'm used to sometimes I don't recognize them until they remind me who they are. I smile and giggle at Jessie to let her know that I am having fun. That's my best answer. She says, "It sounds like you're having fun. I thought maybe we could play together here too. Your dad told me how much you like water and after yesterday I found out myself. Would you like to swim with me?"

Yeah right that's not going to happen. I cling to Daddy and then jump back underwater. I swim with Daddy. Sometimes he'll switch with Mommy, but I won't swim as long with her. There's no way I'm swimming with therapy lady. Daddy tries to slowly back up so I have to cling to her instead, but I just swim after him – sheesh, swimming is easy, it's not like I can't follow him. Grown-ups never give me enough credit.

I dive back under and do a somersault. That's fun! Have you ever done a somersault underwater? You don't know which way is up and which way is down for a little bit. When I open my eyes Jessie is underwater too - watching me. She waves and smiles so bubbles pop out of her mouth. I surface and so does she. I go under and she goes under. Hey, if she wants to play like that it's fine. I bet she gets tired first though. I'd live in here if Daddy would let me.

The Fog Within

She stays with us, talking to me when I surface and following me under when I dive. At first it was annoying, then it was funny, then I got bored and ignored her. She started to breathe heavy like you do when you run and left after a while, waving to us as she went into the bathroom, locker room, smelly pee room. I was glad she left. Not because I don't like her. She's all right for a grown-up, but I was tired. I didn't want to get out before her. After a few more dives I pulled myself out of the pool and yelled, "Dat!" at Daddy until he followed me. Tahbey didn't want to leave, but I was ready so we went. I guess it isn't fair that we don't get to do things because Mommy and Daddy are afraid of the fog. But if they don't do things the way I want then I can't control the fog. I wish the fog wasn't there. I wish Tahbey could play as long as he wanted because it isn't fair to him, but I need to go, and I need to go now, or the fog will push on me and everyone will get upset … not just Tahbey. It isn't fair … but it's the fog. It's never fair.

Chapter Twelve

School was school when I had to go back after my two days off. The kids had stopped teasing me about my accident last week when one of the teachers heard them doing it and he yelled at them like Daddy does when Daddy gets mad. The other kids were scared. I didn't want them to be scared because of me. That isn't fair either. The fog hurts everybody around me sometimes. They might not have been laughing the mean laugh and teasing me if the fog hadn't kept me from using the toilet in time. I was sad that they got yelled at because of me. I didn't want them to get yelled at. I only wanted them to not laugh the mean laugh at me. But then the head teacher … principal? Yes, the principal started yelling at the teacher telling him he can't yell at the students. They sent the kids back to their room, but I stayed and watched because they were mad because of me. I didn't know if I was in trouble or not, or if they were going to call Daddy or not. The teacher and the principal yelled in that grown-up quiet yell they use out at stores and school and places where you aren't supposed to yell. They said some of those bad words and before the teacher stormed off he says to the principal, "They were making fun of her for something she can't help, and if your fucking school board and administration doesn't like the poor, precious, pampered, little angels being yelled at, and the parents want to sue then fine. Bring them down here and have them look Megan in the eyes and say how it isn't fair that their children got yelled at for teasing her. Yeah that makes sense. Jesus Christ! What the fuck is wrong with people?" The principal walked me back to my room after the teacher left still talking to himself like Daddy does. The principal looked sad too. I wish I didn't make people look so sad. I want them to be happy.

The rest of the school day vanishes in a flash. I don't remember it.

When I got home that therapist lady Jessie was there with Mommy. She said she had some games she wanted to add to my touch computer so I could use it at home the same way I had been doing in her office. Mommy and Daddy said they were going to take Tahbey on a walk so he wouldn't bother us. He was already climbing up on Jessie's lap and trying to get her to read him a book. So Daddy scooped him up and says to me, "Have fun kiddo," and they left me alone with Jessie.

I wasn't sure if I liked that I was seeing the therapist lady again outside of her office. It made me start to wonder if she was really there at all. Maybe she was just the fog. Maybe the therapist lady Jessie wasn't real? Maybe she had been the fog playing tricks on me the whole time. The fog can be mean like that – just when I kind of start to like something the fog takes it away, or shows me that it was never there to begin with. There or not she had my touch computer and she was opening up different games, so if she wasn't real then at least I could use the fog to play a game instead. Make the fog work for me for once. I sat down next to her and touched her hair to make sure she was real. It felt like real hair ... but the fog can lie about how things feel too, like touching the bricks on recess.

She smiled and brought up a game similar to the water not water one. It was swirling and moving colors. Red blending to orange, to yellow, to green, to blue, to purple, and different shades in-between. It was pretty, not as awesome as the water game, but nice. I moved down closer to her on our couch to watch the colors for a minute, but then I picked up a magazine and started to flip through it instead. Jessie says, "Wait Megan, that's not all it does, watch." She tapped the screen and the colors rippled like the water, colored water, kind of like Kool-Aid or Jell-O. But it wasn't just movement. Where she touched it played music. I know there are different instruments in music, but I don't know all the grown-up words and names that go with them. I tapped the screen and the colors moved and the banging sound played. The one you hear when you tap on a pot or pan. I touched it again and the colors rippled and the thing with strings played a twanging sound.

It wasn't the relaxing, boring music either. It was the music they play with the mumbled words only there weren't any words. I touched the screen again, rapidly in different places and it started to blend together, pounding and twanging, sounding like a song. I played: one, two, three … only three songs before she reached over and brought up the picture word menu again. Sheesh – of course. She showed me a picture with a bunch of instruments and pressed it. The computer says, "Music Game." Jessie says, "See Megan, if you want to play the music game all you need to do is press the picture for it and the computer will tell me what you want."

Yeah, but since I know how to open the music game it's just easier for me to do it than to go through the effort of pressing the music game button. I growl at her and bring the music game back up. She lets me play a song and then she reaches over and brings up the picture menu again. She doesn't say anything, so I go back to the music game. She lets me play another song and then she reaches over and brings up the picture menu again. I growl. I know what she wants, but I don't want to cooperate. Why should I? I don't need her help, right? I can do it myself. So I go back to the music game. She lets me play another song and then she goes back to the picture menu. Now she's making me mad and I don't want to play the stupid colored music game anymore. The fog is there. I can feel it, hovering, waiting to push me over the edge. I growl and start to bounce up and down on the couch.

Jessie says, "I don't know what you want, Megan. I need you to ask." She gestures toward the touch computer. She's lying. She knows what I want. But, I figure she's in my house so I don't have to listen to her. I reach over to her stupid picture menu but I don't touch the music game button. I flip through the pictures and touch the one of me and the one that means mad. I jump off the couch and run down to my room where I slam the door right after the computer says, "Megan mad."

Chapter Thirteen

Daddy says I'm twelve now. I still don't know how that works. I was just eleven yesterday. How am I twelve today? Numbers are fun, but how am I a number? Lots of people came over to our house: my grandparents, my aunts and uncles, my other family people that have names (I only see them a few times a year so I don't know their names), a few of my friends from school, the weird boy Bobby who lives next door and kind of wanders in and out of the house every day anyway. They brought me gifts to open and we ate cake. I don't know why I get new stuff when my number changes, but the grown-ups seem to think there's a reason so I'll take new toys … and socks … I love socks! I only got one, two, three pairs though, so not as good. I ate the frosting off my pieces of cake and gave the rest to Tahbey. He ate more cake than anybody else. He had some smeared in his hair. It looked funny so I giggled and Tahbey kept asking, "What Megan? What funny?" Mommy cleaned him up once she noticed it.

Everybody says, "Happy birthday, Megan!" when they see me. I smile. That's nice. I'm glad they're happy and they know my name so they probably want me to be happy too, but the rest of it I just don't get. But why waste food and gifts when you don't understand what's going on? There's food there, so eat it. I eat it. I like food. There are presents there for me, so I open them.

The fog gets distracting when I'm in a crowd like that. It's hard. I don't know what to believe is real and what's the fog. Voices that would normally be quiet if it were just a few people get louder in a crowd. Sometimes the fog makes the voices sound louder than they really are. Not good louder either, bad louder. I can feel the fog pressing in while everybody is talking too loud. I grab my touch computer and bring up the picture game, but I can't find a picture that looks like what I want. I can't find a button for "Shut up people! Shut up!" So I try the picture of me, the Megan button, and I touch the mad button. Somebody says something. I don't know who or what because the fog is swimming in my head, swirling with too much noise, too much loud…

…Loud, quiet, want quiet! Where? Home? Bedroom? Quiet! Stop, no, no, yes, quiet. Shut up! Don't go, stay. Not alone, but quiet…

…Daddy's sitting on my bed rubbing my back while I lay on my stomach. When did I get down to my room? I can hear a few voices downstairs, but it is a lot quieter than it was. The fog must have scared everyone away. I must have scared them away. I just wanted them to talk quieter, not leave. I wanted them to use the inside voices that teachers are always going on about, not run away and leave me here with

Daddy. Always me and Daddy. I love him, but it's nice to see other people too.

I sit up in bed and Daddy stops rubbing my back. He says, "You okay, MC?"

"Yeah," I say. See I told you sometimes the simple words come out. I wish I could do that more often. If the simple words broke through the fog more times than not things wouldn't be so hard. I don't like hard. I like easy. Daddy smiles and hugs me. He says, "Good, I'm glad to hear you say that. You want me to bring you some more cake?"

I make the sign for computer. He laughs and says, "I figured," as he reaches down and pulls it out from under his feet. I start to pull up the color music game, but I stop and open the picture menu instead. I find the picture of me and the one for sad (the face on it is frowning and blue - like I said blue sad, not red) and press them. The computer that can talk because I can't, tells my daddy, "Megan sad."

Daddy lies down on the bed next to me and gives me a hug. He says, "That's okay, kiddo. I'd ask you why but I don't think you've figured out how to tell me that yet. I can probably guess though. Don't worry it's okay. Some people understand and some people don't. That doesn't mean that they don't love you, okay?"

I manage to say, "Yeah," again. Daddy hugs me tighter and says, "Besides you've always got me.

I'm not going anywhere no matter how bad you freak out."

I smile up at him. Daddy gets up and then sits down in the big squishy bag chair I have in my room. Beanbag? I looked once and there aren't any beans in it – just tiny white balls that don't taste like anything, especially not beans. I lie back down on my bed. The fog can make me really tired sometimes if I get worked up enough. More tired than if I swam in the pool all day. I don't remember falling asleep, but I must have. I dreamed that the day had started over. Everybody came to our house to see me and they'd say, "Happy birthday, Megan!" again, and they were all happy and smiling.

I didn't know it was a dream ... I didn't know it was the fog being mean. I thought everybody was there again being happy. But then I'd go up to somebody and they'd scream and run away. I'd look for somebody else and when I touched their hand or leg to get their attention they'd scream and run away. I kept chasing after them. I tried to yell, "Don't run away! I'll be good." But the fog choked me. I couldn't say anything. I couldn't even scream. I was running and soon everybody was gone...

...No! Don't go! Megan sorry! Megan wants you to stay! I'm sorry! You can yell! I can yell, scream, kick, cry! We can do anything loud! Don't go, please. Daddy? Where's Daddy? Not alone! Daddy said! There! There's Daddy. I see him. He waves to

me. He smiles, but he starts to fade with the fog. No! No...

...I wake up screaming. I run to my door and turn the knob, but it's locked. I want out. I don't want to be alone. I pound on the door screaming until Daddy stumbles into my room. He says, "Megan honey, what the fuck! It's two o'clock in the morning. What's wrong?"

I grab Daddy and climb up into his arms. He holds on like he did when I was Tahbey's size. Daddy holds me like that for a few minutes but he says, "We have to sit down, kiddo. You're too big for me to carry around like that." He flops down into my not bean chair and holds me until I fall asleep. He's still asleep in the not bean chair when I wake up the next morning.

Chapter Fourteen

I've started to use my picture game menu at school. It doesn't get rid of the fog or anything. It's still there ... waiting. But being able to "talk" to teachers and not teachers helps keep me from being angry when they don't know what's wrong. No more accidents because the teacher thinks I'm trying to get her to take me to lunch. I can touch the button for Megan and toilet, and she'll know what I need. I still get mad if they know what I want but tell me I can't have it anyway. What kind of stupid grown-up thing is that? We want you to talk, Megan. So I do, but when I tell them what I want it's, oh no, you can't do that right now, Megan. The fog seems to wait for moments like that. Moments that don't make sense. Then it pushes harder because I'm keeping it away better.

In the gym, my neighbor's name is Jim too, weird, but in gym the teacher has some of us pull on one side of a rope while more kids pull on the other end. I can't remember what she calls it, but that's what it feels like with the fog now. It's pulling on one end trying to make me act like it wants and I'm pulling on the other trying to act like everybody else without the fog.

I still don't like recess. I tried to play with the ball kids but they only wanted me to run in one direction with the ball when they gave it to me. I thought running in circles would be more fun, so after they took their ball away I went back to my brick wall. The finger tingles are better than running with a ball in a straight line any day.

I can't tell if my teachers like the talking computer or not. Before they just gave me what they wanted to give me and pretended like they didn't know what I wanted – even if they did. But with the computer I can now say, "Meatloaf," over and over and over and over until my teacher gets me meatloaf for lunch instead of picking something else. Or if they do something I don't like I touch "Megan mad" over and over and over too. I also learned to ask "Why?" with the computer when I don't understand something. Jessie showed me how to do that. I ask my teachers why a lot, but they never give me a reason I understand, so I keep asking why. I don't think my teachers like the why button. They still like to talk over me … but I'm catching more and more of what they say when they talk like that.

I see Jessie on some school days and some not school days. I can remember her name now. She's nice. She keeps showing me new words and new games. I even let her swim with me. She was more excited about that than I was. I'm working on combining more than single words together on my computer. Jessie says, "Soon you'll be using full sentences, Megan. I'm so excited!"

She gets excited a lot.

I think sentences are groups of words. Not just one or two like Megan mad, so I'm trying hard to remember how to put them together. I may be able to put five – Five! words together soon. It isn't easy. I know it is for other people, but the fog doesn't want me to be able to do it. The fog wants to keep me quiet. The fog doesn't want me to have a life. It wants me to be alone with it and be sad. But I'm fighting the fog. I have what Jessie calls a goal. Like when the boys who run straight with the ball pass a certain point they yell, "Goal!" It's like that. I want to tell Daddy, "I love you," with more than a kiss. I want my computer voice to tell him. I don't think the fog will ever let me say it with my mouth, but with the computer … I might just do it.

Part II:

Adolescence

Chapter Fifteen

Junior year of high school has been my favorite so far. I only have one more to go, but I don't think it will be better than this year. I think it will be a sad year when it's my last year of school. I know my friends are going on to more school. I can't remember what they call it … it sounds like those big picture collections we used to make in art class where you cut out small pictures and put them on a big sheet of paper. Those are collages. That's close, it sounds like it, but it's not that. My best friend Abby is going to one of those. She's gone on a few trips to look at those *other* schools, because she wants to go to a school far away from home. I don't know why. She doesn't like her home. She doesn't get along with her mom and her dad left when she was a little girl. But Abby is at our house as much as she is at her house, so she'd be leaving us too. She calls my dad, Papa Cooper. She's like having a friend and a sister at the same time, since I only ever had my little brother Todd.

Abby's on the swim team with me. We both love to swim. She doesn't understand what water does to the fog, but she doesn't have the fog either. She's lucky. She just loves to swim because it's fun. I love the water and swimming not only because it helps quiet the fog, but now loving the water has given me a friend too. Not a friend like Sally the brown haired girl from my elementary school. She was sent to a different school when I moved on to the middle school. She had seizures and other physical problems the school I went to was not equipped to handle. With the help of my talker, that's what we all call whatever I'm using to talk with, sometimes it's a computer, sometimes it's a program on my phone, or something else. Any time I use a computer of some kind to talk my parents, doctors, therapists, teachers, and anybody I might be forgetting they call it a talker.

The talker isn't really my voice. It's me. It's what I'm thinking … as best as I can communicate. I left the pictures for sad and mad behind a few years ago and started to type in the words I wanted to say instead. The fog still fights my focus. It doesn't want me to talk to people, even if I "talk" in short bursts and it's not always the words I meant like collage … but it's better than not talking at all. I can talk to Abby and she can talk to me – even if my voice sounds like a girl C3PO when it comes out of the talker. I think C3PO is a boy. I'm not sure. He isn't a Muppet – which I still don't like – but he doesn't wear clothes or have hair or anything to let you know if he's a boy or girl. He gets excited like a lot of girls I know. So, maybe C3PO is a girl? I'll have to remember to ask Dad later. He'll know.

I'm excited because tomorrow will be my first varsity swim meet. Dad and Mom were both worried when Abby said she wanted me to go out for the swim team with her when we started high school. She talked them into it, saying she would look out for me and that I was a good swimmer. I was a good enough swimmer to be on the team and maybe win some meets. I didn't know what she meant at first. I was just happy that she wanted me to swim with her. Mom and Dad were still unsure if I should go out for a sport. Abby even whined to convince them as she said, "Come on Papa Cooper! She needs to do this. She wants to do this. She can do this. Please let me help her."

Dad laughed his sad laugh, took his glasses off, and pinched at that place between his eyes where there are always marks from his glasses. I think he was trying not to cry. When he took his hand away his eyes were red but not wet. He pointed at Abby and said, "Okay, but I need your word, Abs. I need you to promise me that you're going to watch out for her. If I'm not there, then you're me. You got that? I need you to make sure she's okay, that she's not flipping out, that she takes her afternoon medication, that nobody takes advantage of her, that she doesn't get pissed off and leave the pool without calling me, that she-"

"I got it, Papa," Abby said interrupting him. She smiled and added, "I have to be Superdad. I got it." She gave Dad a hug and said, "Thanks."

I ran over and hugged them both. I typed into my talker, "Thank you Dad. I love you!"

103

The Fog Within

"I love you both," Dad said and pushing us away he started to cook dinner. He glanced over his shoulder at Abby and said, "I assume you're staying for supper, Abs?"

I met Abby in junior high. She sat next to me one day and started talking. I used my talker to tell her my name and that I couldn't talk very well or as fast as she could because I had autism and some other things the doctors said, but I didn't know how to type them. She didn't care. She kept sitting next to me ... and she kept talking, and talking, and talking. It was nice to have a friend who didn't care about the fog, and you should hear her if somebody says something mean around me. She uses all those bad words Dad and Mom use when they're mad, and a whole bunch more I'd never heard before. One time freshman year, on the first day we tried out for the swim team, some older boy made a rude comment when he saw me come out of the locker room. I still never know what's a good word or bad word, or when people are saying mean things about me or somebody else. People say a lot of bad words and are mean to each other a lot. It makes me sad that people are so mean all the time. I wish more people were happy. If I can't tell that they're being mean by their laugh or their eyes, I watch to see how Dad, Mom, or Abby react. The boy who said the mean comment didn't know that the swim coach was standing behind him, so when he saw me walking toward the pool in my swimsuit he said, "Oh come on. What is this, the Special Olympics?"

He laughed and his friends laughed. It looked like the swim coach was going to yell at him but Abby stormed over first. She was almost a foot shorter than he was, but she yelled, "You're a piece of shit, and if anybody here is special it's you asshole!" And then she punched him so hard in the face that he fell backwards into the pool. Everybody laughed but me. I didn't want people to be mad or hurt because of me. I didn't want Abby to get in trouble. The coach yelled and had to hold Abby back from the ladder because she was trying to kick the boy in the face while he tried to climb out of the pool. Abby calmed down after the coach told the boy that he had heard everything and he needed to apologize to me. The boy did and the coach let both Abby and me stay. He said we were good swimmers and he wanted us on the team. When we were getting dressed after practice Abby asked me, "Do you think that's what your dad would have done?"

I didn't want to take my talker out near the pool. So during practice I couldn't say much, but once I was in the locker room I had my voice back. I typed, "No, the boy wouldn't have said anything if Dad were there."

"Oh," she said and looked kind of sad and embarrassed. I typed, "But when you tell him about it, I bet he laughs and says you did a good job."

He did too. Mom was worried that Abby would get in trouble, even when we told her the coach wasn't upset. Dad kept laughing, while Mom worried, but I think everything turned out okay.

That was two years ago. A year is how long it takes the Earth, the planet not the dirt, to travel around the sun. I am seventeen years old. It's nice to understand that. The numbers and what they mean, besides just being numbers, were very confusing when I was little. The fog is still with me. I think it will always be with me. It doesn't yell and scream at me like it used to. The fog has found that whispering distracts me more – that it can't push me over into a fit if I have to wait in line, or follow some silly rule the adults around me make up. So, it whispers, it distracts, it still takes whatever it can from me. I still hate the fog.

I take different pills to help with the fog: yellow pills, white pills, blue pills, some pills are round, others are ovals, or capsules to swallow. New pills, old pills, red pills, blue pills. Somewhere the fog turned my life into a Dr. Seuss story. I asked Dad if I could have an extra blue pill tonight so I could sleep. The fog still wakes me up, or keeps me from sleeping, but it wasn't the fog that was keeping me up. Tomorrow was going to be my first varsity swim meet, not just sitting on the sidelines. Abby calls that bench warming. Abby and I are the best swimmers at our school, now that some of the older kids have moved on. It's nice to be good at something and be like other people who don't have the fog. Using a talker isn't like other people, losing focus and pieces of my day isn't like other people, having to have somebody else drive you everywhere because it isn't safe for you to drive isn't like other people, but, playing a sport where other people cheer you on, where other people tell you that you did a good job (and not in that super-happy I'm talking to a person who may not be all there voice people have used with me for years) but talking like they do with everybody else – like a normal person. The water gave me a chance to be like everybody else, hiding from the fog made me like everybody else, even if it was just in one silly way, one silly chance to be like other people, like being on the varsity swim team.

I suppose one more thing that's changed and made me like other people is that I need an extra pill to get to sleep when I'm nervous about something.

Chapter Sixteen

Wow, there were more people at the swim meet than I expected. A lot more. Abby called it, a quad? I think that was because there were three other teams and ours swimming against each other. I'm not sure. I still like numbers. Numbers make more sense to me than words, but if it's a quad because there were four teams, why don't they just call it a four? It's that area where words and numbers blend. It gets confusing – numbers are numbers, but we use words to say numbers, one can be "one" or 1. I like the number better than the word. It makes more sense to me.

The number of people packed into the stands of the pool was a big number. There were people standing around because there weren't enough places to sit, so I couldn't have counted them anyway. I wanted to. I think it might have quieted the fog some if I could know exactly how many people were in the pool stands, but they kept moving and yelling and talking, making them impossible to count. They were all yelling even though nobody was in the water swimming yet. I still think people talk and yell too much. They take their voices for granted. I don't think I'd talk much even if I didn't have to use my talker. I'm better at listening. Abby tells me that all the time, that I'm the best listener she's ever met. Abby likes to talk a lot, but I don't mind it when she goes on and on. It's easier to let somebody talk and talk without interrupting them when you care about them and they care about you.

"Wow," Abby said, looking around at all the people. We were standing next to the bleachers, out of the way. "There sure are a lot of hot guys here. I hope I don't get camel toe with this stupid Eagle's one-piece riding up my ass." And she pulled at the swimsuit with our backs to the wall so nobody would see her do it.

The eagle is our school mascot. That means it's a symbol for the school. It took a lot of explaining for Dad to get me to understand that. Just like when Abby thinks a boy is good looking she calls them hot. For a year in junior high school I kept thinking certain boys were too warm and they should wear a tee-shirt or maybe go see a doctor because they were sick with a fever. But after a while Abby explained what she meant. That's another reason I love Abby; she's like Dad, if I don't understand a word the first time she says it, or if I miss it because the fog sweeps it away, she doesn't tease me about it. She'll take the time to explain it until I understand and not make fun of me or laugh the mean-eyed laugh at me when I don't know right away what she means like everybody else would. She knows words confuse me, so she tries not to use words that have lots of meanings like *hot* unless she's already explained them to me. I don't know what camel toe is ... it has to mean something else, but sometimes I just ignore the words I hear that I don't think are right, or if somebody is using it in a different way. If it isn't important enough for them to say it again I just let it go.

I typed into my talker, "Four teams. Lots of parents, lots of swimmers, lots of people. Hot and not."

"I know it's a quad, Megan," Abby said rolling her eyes.

I typed, "Four."

"Quad," she said back smiling.

"Four," I typed and shook my head.

Abby smiled and hugged me. She said, "Fine, a four it is." Then she pointed up to the stands and said, "Look I can see your mom, dad, and Todd." She waved and yelled across the pool, louder than all the other people yelling, "Hey Coopers!" Mom smiled and returned a small wave, Todd waved and laughed, Dad waved and yelled back in his loud voice, louder and deeper than Abby's, than anybody's I know, "Hey Abs, Hey kiddo! Good luck!"

Some people laughed, others looked like they might be scared of Dad, like maybe Dad had something wrong with him like the fog because he shouldn't yell louder than them. They were yelling first and nobody else should yell louder than their agreed upon level of yelling. I could see it in their eyes. I didn't like their eyes. But Abby and Dad didn't seem to care; they ignored the eyes and kept on being loud. Todd smiled and yelled, "Good luck!" after Dad did. Todd is in the fourth grade and he still follows Dad around and does whatever Dad does.

The crowd was really loud while the boys swam first. Sometimes we alternate boys' events then girls' events because some of the swimmers do lots of different races like I do. It gives them a break. But with so many people there for the four, the coaches decided that the girls' team would swim after the boys, so we had to wait through all the noise. I normally like it that way because half of the parents leave after the boys are done. It lessens the overall yelling level, but with so many people at the four meet the yelling was making the fog press harder on me. The swim coach had only let me practice with the team before in my first two years of high school. It wasn't until this year that I was able to focus enough that he felt confident that I wouldn't get lost in the fog during a meet, and he decided I could participate. The extra loud pool had me worried. I could hear the fog whispering…

…Loud, Megan, too loud? Need to yell back? Need to pull hair? Need to hide?…

The Fog Within

…No, I wasn't going to embarrass Mom, Dad, Todd, and Abby like that. No, I had come too far to let the fog take swimming from me, too. The fog hates that I've found a place it can't hurt me, that I can hide from it, that it can't make me do things I don't want to do. I can't hide the noise of the crowd though, but I can change the noise. Dad bought me a pair of headphones that block out every sound but the song I'm listening to. I dug them out of my bag and turned them on. There fog, take that…

…Maybe this time, Megan, but I'll wait. I'm not going anywhere…

…The music pushed the fog back and it couldn't touch me. I watched the crowd yell and cheer. Their mouths moved and their hands clapped, but all I heard was the music. I've gotten better at understanding the mumbled words with the music, and I still like rock over classical.

When the boys were done and almost half of the crowd had left, Abby tapped me on the shoulder to get my attention. After I pulled my headphones off she said, "Come on, it's show time!" I put my headphones away with my talker and my friend Bobby from next door watched our bags for us, so nobody would take my talker or Abby's purse and stuff. Bobby does that kind of thing a lot for us.

I wasn't as nervous as I thought I'd be when I stripped out of my warm-ups and walked out to the pool. I didn't really care that all those people still in the stands were watching me and the other girls swimming. What I didn't like were their eyes, not the watching – the eyes, but I love the water and I love to swim. If people want to watch me ... who cares? The fog does, that's who. I knew that if I made it to the point where I could get into the pool, the point where the race started, without the fog pushing me over I'd be fine. I just had to get started and not let all the eyes bother me.

Abby and I swim different types of races. That's all school swimming is really just racing in the water with certain rules like: stay in your lane (I had trouble with that one at first, even with those floaty things it's hard to think of there being lines in water – it's water it goes everywhere – lines are straight), swim a certain way (again I had trouble with that: Butterfly, Breaststroke, Backstroke – there are lots of B words in swimming), the number of times you swim back and forth was hard to remember, and tons of other stuff too. Before every race, even in practice, both the coach and Abby make sure to look at me, and say, "It's the two hundred medley relay, Megan." Or "It's the hundred freestyle, Megan." Or whatever race it is so I know how I'm supposed to swim. They both wait until I nod my head, so they know that I understood them. Again, I don't take my talker out near the water. They aren't being mean, or pretending like I'm stupid or something. I asked them to do it when I joined the team so if the fog distracts me on the way to the pool, with all those eyes it can be hard, they can remind me what I'm supposed to do so I don't embarrass everybody.

I swim in five different races! Isn't that cool!

Abby and I had a personal best in the relay, which was good, but we came in second (two) out of the four teams overall. I see the numbers in the words. I know what they mean, but I don't really care. We could have been four out of four, and swam the slowest we ever have and I wouldn't care. It's so much fun to be out in the water with my friend like a normal person, to be like a normal girl without the fog, that I don't care one bit how good or bad we do. It made me happy. Some of the other swimmers and their parents were disappointed that we didn't win, or come in first (one) out of four. I wish other people could be happy over small things like being with your friends and not have the fog change things for you. I don't want other people to have the fog like I do. That wouldn't be fair, but maybe if they saw things through the fog for a day or two they might see how happy they really should be when they come out of it.

I looked over at a boy from another school as they were leaving. His dad was yelling at him for not trying harder. I don't understand that. The dad looked mad and the boy looked sad. Why would you join the swim team if it was going to make you mad or sad? Maybe the fog keeps me from seeing why you'd do something like that. Maybe the numbers are more important to some people than others. I like five, but I don't get mad if something doesn't add up to the number I like. I didn't even do that when I was younger and the fog was worse. I felt sorry for the sad boy and his mad dad, especially since my dad was taking all of us out for pizza afterward. Pizza and swimming; how could anybody be sad about that? Maybe the boy wasn't going to get pizza for not trying hard enough.

Dad drove the car jammed full with people. I sat on Abby's lap and Todd sat on Mom's so we could fit in two more of my friends from the swim team and the boy from next door, Bobby. He's a junior like Abby and I are and he kind of tags along with us to places when he can. He doesn't have many friends at school, so he always hangs out with us. I don't care and Todd thinks it's cool that he has a friend who's in high school. One time when Dad thought he was alone with Mom in the kitchen, I heard him say, "It's like we had two kids of our own and started collecting everybody else's cast-offs and misfits. They're good kids and I don't mind them hanging around. They watch out for Megan and that's more than most adults would do. I just wish the kids' own parents would get their heads out of their asses long enough to realize they're missing out."

I wish Abby could just go ahead and be my sister. I don't know how that adoption thing I heard about works, but I wonder if Dad and Mom could adopt her? She already sleeps over at our house half of the time anyway. She could move in altogether. And Bobby is all right, too. He seems sad a lot like the boy whose dad was yelling at him for not swimming harder, but he doesn't need to be adopted. He lives right next door with his dad Jim. He can come over anytime he wants and not when he can borrow his mom's car, or walk like Abby has to.

It was a Thursday night, a school night, but the pizza place was packed anyway. There were lots of people talking and yelling. I wanted to jam my hands over my ears the second we walked in. I had put on my headphones instead until we got our food, so people wouldn't stare at me. People ignore headphones, but if I cover my ears and rock or make noises to drown out the yelling, people will stare at me. I didn't want to miss out on what Abby and the other girls were talking about. I wanted to be a part of things. They were laughing and giggling about stuff, like certain boys being hot, and Mom and Dad were talking to Todd and Bobby about the new video game they both liked … but if it had just been them I would have been okay. I could have typed in on the conversation. But it wasn't just them, there were dozens of other people talking and yelling in a room smaller than the pool. I watched everyone talk while I waited for the pizza – alone, but not. I smiled, but I had to keep the music turned up. Every time I turned it down the fog would whisper…

...Loud in here, isn't it, Megan? Too loud? Too many people? Maybe you should wring your hands together, or better still, rock in place and make some noises that will make the other people look at you. That would be good, wouldn't it? Show the other people what noise is really like, Megan...

...No it wouldn't be, so I turned my music back up and when Dad looked over at me, I typed, "Too loud, sorry," into my talker and he smiled and nodded that he understood. Abby was keeping the other girls busy with talk about hot guys so I didn't feel too out of place. When the waitress brought the pizza I was able to focus on my food and not the noise, so I put my headphones away. The fog tried...

...Still too loud, Megan?...

...No, I had pizza to eat. I could eat five pieces if I wanted to because some of my pills help keep me from wanting to run around. Besides, I was tired from swimming so the five pieces of pizza would stay down and I wouldn't throw up.

Dad dropped the other girls off at their homes and Bobby went back to his house when we got home. Abby planned to spend the night. Tomorrow was Friday, so she'd probably just sleep over at our house the whole weekend too. It's nice having a friend as close as a sister. I wish she wasn't going away to another school after next year.

Chapter Seventeen

I only have a few classes with the other kids at school. Then I take my work to my special teacher in her special classroom. People use the word special around me so much I wonder if the word is still special if you use it all the time. I thought special meant something that wasn't common, but if the word is used all the time then isn't it common? They also use all kinds of letters that mean several words. My special teacher helps me with my regular schoolwork in an LD classroom. I hear so many of those letter words, initials I think they're called: LD, ADHD, MRDD, MR, NOS, IEP, ABA, and on and on. I know those letter words ... initials, Megan, initials ... I know those initials all mean something, but I really don't care. I still haven't told anybody about the fog. I want to, because they could throw away all their silly grown-up initials and just call it the fog like I do, and it would save a lot of time.

It's not a bad way to go to school though. I do my best to sit through the regular classes, sometimes with Abby, or other times with Wendy and Brittney (the other girls from my swim team). Then I take the work from that class to my special teacher and she goes over it with me again to make sure I understood it. If I have any questions I can ask her using my talker. I take both my talker and my phone with me to all my classes. I'm the only student allowed to use their phone during class. It's supposed to be so if I need something I can ask with it if my talker isn't working, or if I need to focus on something else for a second like the water app I used as a little girl if I feel the fog creeping up on me. Most days I just use it to send a message to Dad because I'm bored. I send, "English Literature is boring," and the teacher thinks I'm doing something to keep the fog away.

Dad sends back, "Not all of it. Pay attention and maybe you'll find something that isn't boring."

"*Romeo and Juliet* is boring, Dad," I send. "Who cares, too much blah blah blah. The words are all mixed up. If the words are supposed to mean something else, then they should say what they mean and not something else to confuse the reader. The writer should just come out and say what they mean. Not use stupid symbols like our school mascot."

"Ask Mrs. Jacobs," he sends back. Mrs. Jacobs is my special teacher. Dad's wrong though. She won't be able to explain the words that are confusing me. She'll try. She'll do her best, but she gets upset when I keep asking her why. Dad would be able to explain it better. I was about to send him that exact message when he sent one to me saying, "If she can't don't worry about it. I'll tell you when you get home."

Dad knows me better than anyone. I don't spend as much time with him as I did when I was little and the fog kept me from talking to him. I have friends my age now. I like to do things with them like swimming, listening to music, or just hanging out. But, I still know he's always there if I need him. Mostly because he tells me it over and over too. "Let me know if you need me, Megan." "Don't worry about it, Megan. I'm here." "If you need me, you know where to find me." I hear at least some version of that several times a day – every day of the week.

I always smile and say, "Yeah, yeah." That's one of the few words I don't need my talker for. I can still say yeah or nah, for yes or no. If I work real hard at it, I can say Dad and not Dat and Mom sounds real close when I try, but I make a u sound instead of an o - Mum. Dad says that's okay, I'm just being British – I don't get it, but I'm not going to ask him to explain it either. He's still weird. I can't say Todd, so every now and then I'll call him Tahbey just to annoy him. He'll say, "Megan, that's a baby name. I'm not a baby anymore!" He isn't but it's still fun to tease him.

School days are still long for me. There is just something so hard about sitting in one place for so long. The fog constantly wants to pull me away. Not just physically and make me throw a tantrum I won't remember doing like in grade school, but now it wants me to stare at something out the window and forget where I am for an hour or more. It's not always easy to fight it off, because most of the time I don't understand what it is they are trying to teach me at school. Why it's important that I know these things. I don't care who started a war before I was born. It's over now isn't it? We're safe, so why do I need to know about it? Or why I need to know the names of all the Presidents? That's silly, most of them are dead ... I think. Maybe that's just the fog making things seem stupid when they aren't. I don't know. I hate the fog, but sometimes when the day is dragging on I kind of miss when I was little and the fog would take away a chunk of my day and I wouldn't realize it. I sit in class most days bored and the fog whispers...

...Bored, Megan? Yell Megan, run around the room, Megan. That wouldn't be boring would it? Run, yell, scream, rock, shake, move!...

...I ignore it, but it's hard. I look forward to swimming and if I freak out at school, if I do what the fog wants me to do, I won't be able to swim afterwards. Dad and Mom say that as long as I don't have too many behavior problems I can keep swimming with the other kids, but, if I give in to the fog, if I scream and yell like it wants me to then I won't be allowed to swim.

So I go through my day, from one regular class then back to my special teacher, and back and forth and back and forth. Until the day is over and I'm about ready to freak out, then it's into the water – swim, float, glide, hide from the fog, be a fish not a person with the fog, be movement, be motion, for a few hours out of my day just ... be.

Chapter Eighteen

I was wrong. Abby didn't stay over at our house for the weekend. Wendy's mom said it was okay for her to have a sleepover with the girls from the swim team, so Abby wanted us to go there instead. I don't know all of the girls as well as I know Abby, Wendy, and Brittney. Dad was worried about me going. Mom had already left for work so the decision was up to Dad. Whining and begging, Abby said, "Please, Papa Cooper. I promise to look out for her Superdad style. I promise I'll beat the shit out of anybody if they say anything or do anything wrong. It's just a sleepover. I promise!"

Dad laughed at her. He was probably thinking about freshman year when she hit that boy. I typed, "Please, Dad." It wasn't that I wanted to go. To be honest I was worried. I don't like going to parties. I never have, ever since I was a little girl and the fog was worse. Too many people talking too loud can cause the fog to come crashing in hard and fast, losing control at a party was and is too easy. I could and would take my headphones but if I sat in a corner listening to music all night what would be the point in going in the first place. But, Abby wanted me to go, so I wanted to go. She's always had that kind of influence on me. She makes me feel like I don't have the fog sometimes, like I'm not some freak, like I am a normal girl with a friend, a girl who goes to sleepovers. So I typed again, "Please, Dad."

He shook his head, but said, "Fine, just make sure you take your pills and get some sleep. Don't stay up all night, and you," he pointed at Abby, "make sure she takes her pills and doesn't stay up all night."

"Yeah, yeah," we both said at the same time and laughed.

Wendy's house was a lot bigger than my house. She had a bedroom the size of my living room. I like my smaller rooms. The big rooms made me feel like I was at school, or a museum, or someplace else people are only supposed to visit, but not live in. All the girls from the swim team were there and a few more too. There were a lot of girls I didn't know. I wanted to leave the second I realized how many people really were there, hiding in different rooms, playing loud music, kissing and hugging. There were a lot of boys there too. I didn't see Wendy's mom or dad anywhere. I pulled on Abby's arm and typed, "I thought this was a sleepover?"

"It is, Megan. We're going to sleep here ... but it's more like a party than a sleepover," she said. "Don't worry, if you need to go outside or something to get a break just let me know and I'll go with you. If somebody offers you a beer, don't drink it. I don't know how your medications will react to

123

alcohol, and your dad would kill me if something happened."

"Fine," I typed, but I don't like parties and I was starting to want to go home. I didn't want Abby to be upset with me for wanting to leave, for not wanting to be like a normal girl. I didn't want to be like Bobby from next door and have no friends my age, and have the fog bothering me too - that would be too much. If I was stuck with the fog I needed to have friends too, or what would be the point in fighting the fog. I could just let it pull me under and no one would care.

There were more and more kids showing up the longer we stayed. It was getting way past the point where Dad would tell me to go to sleep, but more people kept coming. I didn't know most of them. There were a lot of boys as well as girls. They were drinking beer and some of them were smoking. I don't mind beer. Dad lets me have one every now and then, but he knows my pills better than I do, so I didn't want to risk it. I don't like smoking though. I don't know why people would want to pull smoke into their mouths. It looks like it would hurt. I lost sight of Abby for a few minutes and started to get worried, but I found her talking with a group of girls and boys I didn't know. I stayed back from the group. I didn't like how all the kids' eyes looked, glazed and happy but confused as if they weren't sure where they were, or maybe like they had a fog of their own to see through. I wanted to keep an eye on where Abby was, but I didn't want to interrupt her. New people react weird sometimes to the fact that I use a talker and don't speak. If I'm with Dad I know nobody will say anything mean. Abby might beat somebody up for being mean, but people don't know that until it's too late. I didn't want her to get in trouble because of me and the fog and how people react to us. That wouldn't be fair.

I needed to go to the bathroom. I held it for a while, but I had to pee really bad, so I left Abby where she was having fun, talking to the group of people I didn't know and went looking for Wendy's bathroom. I had to go upstairs and down a long hallway before I found it. People were in all the bedrooms kissing and hugging every time I opened a door like that annoying *Romeo and Juliet*. I found the bathroom. It was as big as my bedroom. After I peed, I went looking for Abby and couldn't find her. She wasn't where she was before. The group of people she had been talking to were gone. I tried to send her a message with my phone, but she didn't answer. I looked for ten minutes and started to get scared. I didn't know any of the people at the supposed to be sleepover. It was Wendy's house and I couldn't find Wendy. I looked out back where a few kids were smoking and pouring beer down a plastic funnel into some guy's mouth – weird. I started to get scared…

…Megan scared? Megan should yell, scream, or cry. Maybe Abby will come if Megan screams?…

The Fog Within

...I didn't scream, but I also didn't know where I was. The fog had distracted me enough that I had left Wendy's house. I was walking down a sidewalk I had never been on before. Abby had borrowed her mom's car to drive us there and I didn't know where my house was from Wendy's. I didn't recognize any of the houses I was walking past. The houses looked like faces – sad faces. Sad faces with sad eyes, sad, worried, scared eyes...

...Sad scared faces with sad scared eyes, Megan. Eyes that are being mean to you. You know that don't you, Megan? Eyes that want to hurt you. Eyes that make you want to run, to scream, to cry...

...I don't remember where I went. I may have run. I may have screamed, but when the fog left me alone enough to think, to look at where I was, I realized I was walking down the middle of a busy street, following the yellow lines, staying in my lane like the swim coach wants me to, and cars were flashing their lights at me. People were honking their horns, yelling bad words at me, and calling me names...

...They don't like you, Megan. They don't want to be around you. You scare them. You make them sick. You are alone. Where's Daddy now? You need Daddy. You are too weak on your own. Scream, Megan, scream!...

...I woke up and heard Dad yelling. He was yelling in that loud scary voice where it sounds like

126

his voice has been switched with the bass keys on a piano. When he yells like that it feels like he is sucking all the air out of the room and you are so scared you can't breathe, even if he isn't yelling at you. He wasn't yelling at me. I had my face buried in the couch, but I could hear him yell, "God damn it, Abs! What the fuck were you thinking letting her out of your sight? You promised me! Fuck that! You promised *her*! You want to lie to me fine. People lie to each other all the goddamn time. But you promised Megan you'd look out for her like I do, and she was almost hit by a car! Fuck, if Bobby's dad Jim hadn't been going out for a late night Taco Bell run and spotted her, I don't want to think about what would have happened. I've never been so happy for fast food in all my life. Thank God my neighbor's heart is as big as his ass!"

I turned my head and looked into the kitchen. Dad was standing with his arms crossed while Abby sat at the table crying. It was still night, so chances were Dad hadn't called Mom at work. He'd try to keep her from finding out, because if she had been home she never would have let me go in the first place. Mom doesn't trust the fog. Dad doesn't either, but he wants me to be normal so bad sometimes he gives in when he shouldn't, like tonight. Sometimes things work out and I get to have fun and pretend I'm normal, and sometimes like tonight, the fog messes everything up. Abby was crying so hard I could barely understand her when she said, "I'm sorry."

"Sorry?" Dad yelled, uncrossing his arms and running them through his hair. "Jesus! Sorry, sure no shit you're sorry. Let me guess, you were flirting with some guy and you lost track of where she was? Abs ..." he stopped yelling and started talking as he leaned over the table, "... damn it kid, I know you don't have shit for an example at home, but come on! If you wanted to do the whole hormonal teenager thing you should have said so, and just told Megan it was going to be a party to begin with. You know she hates parties. It wouldn't have been a big deal for you to go by yourself."

Abby's crying slowed down a little and she looked up at Dad and said, "But I want her to get to do things like other kids. It isn't fair. She isn't that crazy, Papa. She's a lot smarter than people think."

"And you think I don't know that, Abs? You think I don't want the same damn thing?" Dad said, almost whispering. No longer yelling and sucking the air out of the room. "But I've had seventeen years to learn she isn't like other kids. She never will be, but that's what makes her who she is. Why she's so special, because she's one of a kind. But there are some things she can do and there are some things she can't do. That's the way it is, and if you love her like I do then you just have to accept those limitations. You have to figure out which is more important to you; spending this last year with her and having fun like you did as kids, or are you going to start growing apart now? She can't go to college with you, Abs. You know that, and," Dad paused and pulled a chair out next to Abby, sat down, and squeezed her hand as he said, "I understand why you want … why you need to run as far as you can. I know you need to start fresh somewhere that nobody knows you, that doesn't have some bad memory attached to it … but, you aren't just running from your mother. You're running from us too, from Megan. When you leave it's going to crush her. We both know that. Megan knows you're leaving, but she doesn't know. She understands, but she doesn't."

Abby started to cry harder again. Dad patted her hand and stood up. He said, "I'm going to take Megan up to her room and put her to bed. I think we need to talk more, but I'll understand and not think any less of you if you're not here when I come back down."

Dad walked over to me in the living room and smiled. He leaned down and stroked my cheek before he asked, "You okay, MC?"

"Yeah," I whispered as he picked me up like I was still a little girl and carried me upstairs, tucking me into bed he kissed my forehead and said, "No more parties for a while, okay?"

I said, "Yeah," but before I fell back to sleep I thought I heard Abby's car door slam and the engine drive away.

Chapter Nineteen

I slept in really late the next morning. It was a Saturday and after what the fog did to me at the party the night before, I didn't want to move. I wanted to hide under my mattress like I did when I was a little girl. I almost did. I almost ripped everything from my bed and squeezed underneath the huge pile of pillows, blankets, and bedding where I knew it would be safe. Where if the fog found me, it could only whisper and not really hurt me. But I stayed on top of my bed like a normal person. I didn't feel normal, but it was something small that I could control, something small that I could do like everyone else, even if it was just pretend normal.

I could tell it was getting late. The sun was really bright through my curtains when somebody came into my room and sat at the edge of my bed. I didn't know if it was Mom or Todd because my head was turned toward my window. I knew it wasn't Dad because the bed would have sunk a lot further down than it did if it had been him. He also typically sits in my beanbag chair too, not my bed. I didn't know it was Abby until she said, "Are you awake, Megan?"

My head was still turned away from her and I didn't move, but I said, "Yeah."

She didn't move for a while, not even to shift around, and neither did I. She must have been holding her face in her hands because she sounded muffled when she said, "I'm sorry. I shouldn't have taken you to that stupid party last night. I should have known better. I just wanted you to have some fun like everybody else. I ... I don't know..."

I reached over and grabbed my talker from the nightstand where Dad leaves it plugged in for me. I typed, "I have fun, Abby. But not like everybody else. I don't understand what was supposed to be so much fun about last night. Lots of people I don't know talking about other people and stuff I don't know. They don't know me and don't know about the fog. How is that fun?"

"The what?" Abby asked looking over at me.

"It's what I call all the stuff that happens to me," I typed. I hadn't even told Dad that I called it the fog. I had never told anybody that because I was afraid they'd think I was crazier than they already thought. "Once, when I was little, Dad said, 'She's lost in her own fog.' I think of all the things wrong with me as a fog that sweeps in and messes with my head and how I see and feel. It hides the world from me. It hides why last night was supposed to be fun."

"Jesus..." Abby said quietly and hid her face in her hands again.

131

The Fog Within

"I was awake last night when Dad yelled at you," I typed, but she didn't say anything. I was worried that what I'd said about the fog had scared her. I waited but she didn't say anything, so I typed, "I don't understand why you have to leave. Why don't you stay and go to more school here?"

"It's not that easy, Megan," Abby said and she started to cry.

"Sure it is," I typed. "There are lots of schools here. I know I'm not going to go to them, they're for people without the fog, but they're near here. I'm going to try and get a job after next year. I hope I can work at the zoo. You can stay here and go to school and I can work like other adults and we can still hang out."

"Megan, honey … I'm sorry for last night," Abby said as she cried, "but the point that you don't understand why last night was supposed to be fun … well that's why you won't understand why I have to leave next year. I have to get away."

It was one of those moments when I wanted to rip the fog away, to shove it, kick it, punch it, do something to it, to make it leave me alone so I could see the world like other people do … but that's why it's a fog – you can't do anything to it, yet it can take away everything from you.

I think we both knew we had gotten as far as we could about her moving away next year after graduation. She loved me and I loved her, but things would always be different for us. There would always be a distance between us that we couldn't cross. I sat up in bed and hugged her from behind, and Abby started to cry harder.

When she had cried enough that her eyes were really red and puffy, I typed, "It's okay. We'll still have fun this year while you're here, but no more parties, okay?"

She laughed and hugged me again. She said, "Sure thing. No more parties."

We went downstairs and Dad was making pancakes for Todd and Bobby. Bobby stood up really fast and asked, "Megan, are you alright? My dad said he almost hit you with his car last night. Are you okay-"

"Whoa there, Bobby Big Mouth," Dad interrupted him, pointing the spatula at him like a sword. "What did I just say? I talked to your dad already and he's cool, but the only other people that know about last night are in this room right now. Meaning Mrs. Cooper does not, and if the rest of you don't want me pointing fingers and laying blame (trust me, I'll lie through my damn teeth about it. I'll blame it on UFO's if I have to) then you will all keep your tiny teenage mouths shut about it. Put in simple kid terms, 'Last night never happened!' Megan is fine so sit down, shut up, and eat your fucking pancakes, Bobby."

The Fog Within

"Yes, Mr. Cooper," Bobby said as he sat back down, but I smiled at him to let him know I was okay. He smiled back.

After breakfast Dad took all of us to the pool while Mom slept. Dad doesn't swim with me like he used to when I was little, but there is a weight room at the pool that has a window overlooking the water. Dad went with Bobby and Todd to lift weights while Abby and I swam, but every time I looked up either Dad or Bobby was watching us from the window. I know they worry about me. After what the fog did last night I can't blame them. I blame the fog. I'll keep fighting it. I don't want to be lost ... but some days it feels like things would be easier if I just let the fog take me. If I can't understand why my best friend needs to leave me and the people that love her, or why parties are fun, or how to act like other people, or how to talk without a talker, then maybe I should let the fog take me. Let it pull me under forever and never try to come back out...

...Yes, Megan. Forever and ever until death do us part. Yes, Megan I do...

...No, I will keep fighting the fog. It can't have me. I'm me. I'm not the fog. The fog isn't really there. It's just a lie...

...Really, Megan. You don't believe that. We both know it. I'm here and you're there. Only you can't see me. But, oh my, my, my I can see you. I can make you see things, and hear things, and feel things

that aren't there, Megan. I'm real all right, and you know it...

...I swam until I was exhausted, drowning out the fog, and then I swam some more. Abby was done and waiting for me. I didn't get out of the pool until I saw Dad kneeling down by the edge with his hand reaching out to me. He said, "Come on, Megan, honey. I'm here, let's go home."

Chapter Twenty

School goes by fast and school goes by slow. I think most people, even those without the fog, feel that way. It seems like it's dragging on boring you to death while you're there all day long, but then you look back and a month or more has gone by.

The school swimming season is only when it's cold out; a winter sport the coach calls it. I don't care. I swim when I want to swim and whenever I can get Dad or Mom or Abby to take me to the pool. I'm on the team because Abby wants me to be on the team, and the coach does too. He said my form isn't always the best, but he's never known an athlete to put so much of themselves into a sport like I do. I smile and type, "Thanks coach," because I don't think he'd understand if I explained to him about the water hiding the fog. I don't think Abby really understood when I told her. I think maybe the fog works both ways. It keeps me from understanding why certain things are important to other people and all those weird rules they all love, but at the same time I can't explain the fog to them because they don't have it. If I told somebody with the fog why I call it the fog, I bet they'd understand. I've been around some other people with their own version of the fog, but every fog is different. Some fogs are thick and some are thin, some only whisper and some yell, some take away time and others take away movement. No two fogs are alike. I think that makes it hard to explain. Two people can have the fog, but both are lost in different ways, and the people around them don't know how to help pull them out. Some people don't even want to be pulled out of their fog. It hides them and they feel safe. Other people like me want the fog to go away and let them be normal.

My fog took away most of the winter without me noticing. I went to school. I went to swim practice. I went home. Dad helped me with my homework. I might watch Todd and Bobby play a video game, or watch a movie. Abby would come and she would go. Repeat that pattern weekly and my last swim meet was there before I realized it.

Abby and I had been doing good enough at all the meets that we got to swim a week later than the rest of the team. The coach said it was a regional, or sectional, or something. Another word with lots of meanings that really was just us swimming against other swimmers that were good.

My old therapist Jessie even came to the meet to cheer us on. I looked up at the bleachers and I saw more faces that I knew. My grandparents had come to watch, along with Mom, Dad, Todd, and Bobby. Even Bobby's dad Jim was there. He took up the seats of two people, and Bobby kept looking at him like he was embarrassed to sit next to him. I don't know why. I like Jim. He's nice. He's really fat, but really nice. Besides, my dad was holding up a giant sign that said "It's Hammer Time!" so I don't think Bobby should feel embarrassed by his dad.

Because it was a regional, or sectional, or whatever, we had to drive to a new pool I'd never been in before. It had bigger stands set up around it for more people to watch from – for more eyes to watch from. The coach said it was a college pool. That's where Abby's going next year – college. I knew it sounded like collage. The college pool had lots of people yelling and cheering their swimmers on. It was very loud and I could hear the fog whispering…

…Too loud, Megan. Too many people. Look at their eyes, Megan. See how mad, excited, wild, scared, and angry they all are. This is no place for you, Megan. You shouldn't be here. You should scream. Come on, Megan. Scream!…

…I put my headphones on and shut the fog out. I shut all the yelling out until the coach came and found me, hiding under the bleachers, and looked me in the eyes … his eyes were excited … I didn't like that. He said, "Two hundred freestyle relay, Megan. You got it?"

"Yeah," I said and followed him and Abby to the pool. The coach carried our bags because it was so busy Bobby had to sit up in the stands. The college had different rules than the other pools. Only certain people were allowed in certain areas at certain times.

I heard a few people muttering that same comment about it being the *Special Olympics* when they thought we wouldn't overhear them. I didn't want to look in their eyes. I knew I'd see the mean not laughing eyes of the kids on the playground, but grown-up and older, sadder, and madder. I didn't like all the eyes. It had never bothered me that bad before. The eyes are always there. It wasn't that they were watching me that had me upset, but what was in their eyes, in all those eyes, eyes, eyes…

…Anger, excitement, mad, win, scream, win, yell, lose, try harder, lose, swim faster. It's all there, Megan. All in their eyes…

…I do not let the fog pull me under. It was the first time in my life that when I plunged into the water that the fog followed me. It wasn't the fog, but it was. It was the eyes that followed me under. I could see them all as I swam, every eye, even though mine were only open when I surfaced. All the watching eyes were behind my closed eyes. I could see them, feel them, touch them, and hear them.

The eyes didn't affect my swimming. The eyes didn't stop me from hitting a personal best time. But the eyes still bothered me. They bothered me more and more when I got out of the water. The water held the fog back, but not the eyes. Without the water I had both the fog and the eyes to deal with.

When the numbers and times were recorded by all the official adults and they figured out who got what numbers - Abby and I missed going to state our coach said by one place. I guess state comes after regional, or sectional, or whatever. What that really only meant was one less time swimming as a team and back to me swimming by myself, so it wasn't a big deal. The coach said since we swam our best he was still happy and proud of us for doing so well, and he was excited because he thought we'd do even better next year. His eyes agreed with his mouth, but not completely. His eyes also said he was sad and he had hoped we would be going to state. We already lived in a state. There are a bunch of them, so I don't know why going to state was such a big deal.

Our last race had been when the entire event was only halfway over, but I didn't want to stick around and watch the other schools. We had gone back to where I had been hiding under the bleachers before – away from the eyes. I reached into my bag for my talker and typed to my coach, "Can you go get my dad?"

"Sure, Megan," he said and went around the pool, pushing past all the people to get to where my family was way up in the bleachers on the other side. Abby tapped my shoulder and asked, "Are you okay honey?"

"Nah," I said, shaking my head and because I couldn't say the rest I typed, "Eyes, too many eyes. Need to stop seeing the eyes."

140

"Oh, okay sweetie," she said looking nervous and picking up my bag with hers, she slipped her hand under my arm. She waved at my dad across the pool so he'd know where we went as she guided me further under the closest bleachers. We went past where the lights shone under, way back in where it's dark and dirty because no one ever goes under there, but kids and people that are scared and need to hide. Abby said, "We'll just get you someplace where the eyes can't see you. How's that sound? Someplace nice and hidden so everybody can't see you."

I typed, "Not stupid, Abby. Just crazy."

"Oh sweetie, don't," she said and crouched down, helping me put my warm-ups back on over my swimsuit. "I know that. I'm sorry. I just didn't know what else to say."

We were only under there by ourselves for a few minutes when I heard Dad ask, "What's wrong?" He was out of breath. He must have run the rest of the way when Abby waved to him. I typed, "Eyes Dad. Too many eyes. Too much yelling in the eyes."

"Shit!" Dad said. He was leaning down at the edge of the bleachers, still standing in the light, looking in at us. Then he stood up and glanced around at the packed stadium full of people wandering everywhere, some yelling, some cheering, all with loud eyes. He leaned back down and said, "Megan, I don't want to have to carry my teenage daughter out of here Kevin Costner in 'The

Bodyguard' style. I will if I have to, but you're stronger than that, okay? Are you with me, Megan?"

"Yeah," I said, and typed, "eyes are yelling, saying things their mouths don't. The eyes are louder than the mouths."

"Fuck!" Dad said and rubbed his hands over his face, pressing his palms into his eyes. When he took his hands away he looked over at Abby. "Abs, I need you to get the bags and go tell Coach Mitchel what's going on, and then go tell everybody else to meet us in the parking lot. You got that?"

"Sure thing, Papa Cooper," Abby said and grabbed our bags. She was gone and it was just me hiding under the bleachers. Dad climbed in, bumping his head a few times and saying more bad words as he squeezed into the tight space. Then he sat down next to me, putting his arm around me and held my far hand in his. He didn't say anything for a while. He sat next to me and squeezed my hand. I squeezed back. I heard Bobby ask, "Is she okay, Mr. Cooper?"

"Yeah Bobby," Dad said while I looked hard at the dark, dusty floor. "She's just having a bit of an issue with all the people. This may be too much for her to handle. I don't think she's ever been in a crowd this big before. You and your dad can go on home, Bobby. Tell Jim I'll stop by later with a beer and an explanation. Tell him thanks for coming, it meant a lot to her … and it meant a lot to me too, kiddo."

"Sure Mr. Cooper," Bobby said. "No problem, I'll see you later," and then real hesitantly he added, "you did great, Megan. I'm sorry you and Abby didn't qualify for state."

Then it was just Dad and me again under the bleachers. It was dusty, dirty, and dark under there, cramped and pressed beneath all those people. It was strange that a place like that, a place in the dark could be less scary than a place under bright lights like the pool. Dad squeezed my hand again. I squeezed back. I was trying to focus on him, on his hand, but…

…The eyes are out there waiting, Megan. Oh yes they are. Just waiting for you to come back out. They want to yell at you, Megan. The eyes want to scream. You want to scream, don't you, Megan? Scream…

… "Hey MC," Dad said, pushing past the fog. "I have an idea. I know you're hurting right now. I know you're scared and you don't want to go back out there. It's quiet under here…" he looked up at the screams echoing down from the bleachers, "…well, quieter anyway. I know you don't want the eyes to yell at you. I know you don't want me to carry you out of here like a little kid. I know you don't want that."

143

"Nah," I said and kept my face hidden as I typed, "scared."

"I know," he said, "but here's what we do. I can't get rid of the eyes. They're still going to be there no matter what I do, and we aren't going to sit under here for the next two hours and wait for everybody to leave. That would be letting the eyes win. I say fuck the eyes, Megan! Fuck'em all, they don't matter. They're going to stare and yell at you no matter what we do, so just look at my eyes. They aren't yelling."

I looked up from the dirty stadium floor. Dad was smiling at me and his eyes were smiling too. He nodded his head and said, "You with me? I can walk backwards and if anybody has something to say with their mouth, or their eyes, then let them say it to me and not you. Come on, you with me?"

He stood up and carefully ducked out from under the bleachers. His eyes never left mine. He reached his hands out for me to hold and he took small shuffle steps backwards out into the crowd, out of the safe dark and into the scary light. He bumped into a few people and said, "Excuse me," or "Pardon me," as we went, but he never broke eye contact with me. I don't know how he didn't fall backwards into one of the pools. I would have, but he didn't. People watched us, I could tell, but they didn't say anything. I could feel their eyes yelling, but they couldn't shout past Dad's eyes. His eyes were

144

happy, tired, and kind. They weren't yelling. I followed his eyes out of the pool and into the lobby where Abby was waiting with our bags. She said, "Everybody is ready to go, Papa Cooper."

Dad smiled and said, "Good, thank you, Abs. I think Megan is too, right?" I broke eye contact first and looked over at Abby and said, "Yeah."

Chapter Twenty-one

I went swimming at my pool the next day. I was worried that the eyes would follow me into the water, but it must have just been that college pool that the eyes could do that in. Maybe it was because of all those people yelling and screaming, because as soon as I dove in there was nothing but the water. There was only the quiet, soothing rush of water, no fog, no eyes, just calm. Dad had driven me up because he wanted to lift weights with Todd. My little brother wants to play football, so Dad has him lifting weights already even though Todd isn't in junior high yet. I think it's not really about football, but it gives Dad and Todd something they can do together that I'm not a part of, or Mom, or anybody else. Dad doesn't really like video games as much as Todd does. He tries to play them, but Todd likes the ones where it looks like you're in the game and Dad says those give him a headache. So they can lift weights together without Dad getting a headache or Todd getting bored – just the two of them. Unless they invite Bobby along sometimes, maybe it's a boy thing, but picking up a weight over and over and putting it back down in the same place doesn't seem all that fun to me.

Abby loves to swim, but she doesn't have the same need to be in the water that the fog has pressed on me. She said she didn't want to go swimming the day after regionals, or sectionals, or whatever it was that we swam. I don't know why that should matter, but it did for Abby, so I swam alone. It was a Sunday morning and I had the entire pool to myself. There was no lifeguard on duty until the afternoon, like I needed one, but the point is I was the only one in the water. I was the only one in that huge room. I could hear my strokes echo off the walls and the ceiling. I paused and held on to the side of the pool for support, scissor-kicking my legs under me so the echoing stopped. Only the noises coming from the furnace could be heard. I tried to talk. There was no one there to laugh at what came out if it didn't make sense, or if it sounded silly. In the large quiet pool I said, "Me-gan." I had been working on saying my name at every school I've ever been to so it wasn't so hard. I said it again, "Me-gan."

The walls echoed in my voice, "Me-gan, Me-gan."

Then I tried to say the word that would never come out, "Lllluuu."

The walls echoed and mocked me, "Lllluuu."

I wish I could tell Dad that I loved him. I've typed it on my talker hundreds of times, but that isn't the same. He doesn't care, but I do. After my problem at the regionals, or sectionals, or whatever and how he was willing to embarrass himself instead of me being humiliated, I really wanted to tell him with my mouth, not my talker. I wanted to tell him

147

with my voice and not the talker's girl C3PO voice. But, the fog just won't let me. In the echoing, "Lllluuu,"s I could hear the fog whispering…

…Megan, Megan, Megan. You can't talk, Megan. How many times do I have to tell you? I can tell you, but you cannot tell anyone else. Megan, Megan, Megan. I'm the only one you'll get to talk to. Scream for me, Megan. Scream…

…I didn't scream. I went back to swimming to quiet the fog, to quiet the only thing that kept me from speaking, the only thing that kept me from being like everyone else, and I blocked it out with the calm rush and splash of the water.

Chapter Twenty-two

The fog blended the next few months and before I knew it the weather was warming up. That was a good thing because it meant that soon I'd be able to swim outside once the outdoor pools were warm enough or the lakes. I like swimming in lakes too. Also with the warmer weather Dad would be more likely to take us to the zoo on weekends. I love the zoo. Dad lets me wander and look at the animals at my pace while he and Todd, or Abby, or Bobby, or Mom (if she isn't sleeping) go at their pace. I like to stay at the huge floor to ceiling aquarium. I went way past five laps of the zoo the first time Dad let me go on my own. If I remember it right I made it up to fifteen laps, and Dad found me asleep on the bench in front of the aquarium. After that I didn't feel the need to do five laps or more of the zoo. I don't know if that was because of one of my red pills, blue pills, old pills, or new pills, or if it was me growing up and seeing further past the fog, but once I got to do as many laps as I wanted it lost its drive. I had done five and then some, so I started to look closer at the animals, not just the fish in the aquarium, but the big animals too. I like to watch the monkeys play, and the lions pace back and forth, or the elephants eat big sticks and branches. I feel sorry for the lions though and some of the other large animals. The animals that you wouldn't want to meet in the wild. They're trapped in their tiny little pretend homes, with fake rocks, plastic plants, and mown grass. They want to run and be wild, but they're stuck in a box where people talk and laugh at them. They don't know what those people are saying, or why they are laughing.

The large animals remind me of what it was like to be lost in the fog. They're held against their instincts and cannot do anything about it. They make me sad and happy at the same time. Sad for them and happy for me – I can step out of my box most of the time, but they can't.

I was watching one of the female lions stalk back and forth along the far wall of her box. Dad had taken all of us to the zoo one warm day after school. The sad lion kept looking down at her paws as she paced instead of looking up at the people watching her. She didn't want to be reminded that there was a world beyond her feet. If she kept looking down she might be able to pretend her box wasn't real, that she wasn't trapped. It reminded me of when I used to run my hand along the brick wall during grade school recess. I looked away from the lion and down at my fingers where they started to tingle at my side. It made me want to cry. I wished the lion could find a way out of her fake world and be like other lions in the wild. Abby's voice interrupted my thoughts. She was talking to both Dad and Mom. She said, "I want this guy Ryan from over at Central to ask me, but I only want to go to our prom. I don't want to go to his. Most of the kids at Central are just a bunch of potheads. Do you think he'd be okay with that, just going to our prom?"

"I don't know, Abs," Dad said and sat down next to me. "I never went to any of mine. I'm not into that kind of thing."

He smiled at me and I leaned my head on his shoulder. The lion was still making me sad, but I couldn't stop watching her. My eyes kept going back to her no matter how much I wanted to leave her alone. I wondered if her paws were tingling. My mom said, "I think it couldn't hurt to ask him, Abby. He's a guy so he's probably too dense to figure out what you want no matter how much you hint, so just be straight forward and ask him. He probably won't even be listening to you, so you'll have to repeat yourself to make sure he understands."

"What dear?" Dad asked.

"Ha ha," Mom said in a fake laugh. "See what I mean, Abby? If you want to go to prom your way you'll have to take charge. Don't let the boy make the decision, because he never will."

I looked away from the sad lion, pulled my talker out, and typed, "What's prom?"

"It's like homecoming," Abby said, "but just for juniors and seniors, or an underclassman if they go with an upperclassman."

151

"So it's like a party?" I typed.

"No sweetie," Mom said. "It's a dance at the school. People go on a date and get dressed up. They usually go out to dinner first, then they go to the dance, and sometimes they have parties afterwards, but not always."

"So it's a school thing?" I typed.

"No," Dad said, interrupting both Abby and Mom before they could say anything. He didn't turn and look at them. He kept watching the sad lion. Mom asked, "No what?"

"No," Dad repeated. "No it isn't a school thing. It's a party thing and Megan wouldn't like it. I'm more psychic than psychotic ... well, maybe it's a split decision, but still I can see where this is going. Megan honey, you don't want to go to prom, trust me."

"Oh," Mom said. "I hadn't ... I wasn't thinking that, but ... Megan, do you want to go? I mean you could go. They call it going stag and lots of kids do it. It could be fun for her. I don't see how it would hurt if she went to the dance."

"I do," Dad said, "and no."

"But what if she wants to go?" Abby asked. Dad turned around at that. He glared at her for a second and said, "Taco Bell, Abs. Am I clear?"

Abby nodded, but Mom said, "No you're not. You sound like your psychotic beat psychic in overtime. What do you mean 'Taco Bell'?"

"It's slang babe," Dad said. "It means, *No fucking way in hell*. You know kids and their wacky sayings. Hell and bell rhyme and that's enough for them, right Abs?" Dad said smiling at Abby, but his eyes weren't smiling. His eyes were yelling at Abby. I had never seen Dad's eyes yell before. I felt sorry for Abby. She said, "He's right Mrs. Cooper. It probably wouldn't be a good idea. You know how Megan doesn't do well at parties. Remember her fourteenth birthday when she threw the ice cream all over Bobby because she thought the candles from the cake had caught his shirt on fire?"

Dad turned back to the sad lion, but Mom wasn't going to let it go. I could see her clenching her jaw in that way she does when she's mad about something. She said, "Megan has come a long way since then you two. I think if she wants to go to prom she should. It would be nice for her to do some of the things her classmates do and not be a social rebel and outcast like half of her gene pool."

"I'll take her." Everyone turned to see Bobby standing next to Todd. They must have walked up while Mom and Dad were talking and nobody noticed. He looked scared like he always does. I don't know if he wanted to take back what he said or not, but when Dad turned slowly around from watching the lion it looked like Bobby thought jumping into the lions' cage might be a better idea than standing there looking back at Dad. Todd laughed and mumbled, "Dumbass," before he walked over to lean on the railing of the lions' cage. Mom said, "Language Todd," but only with half her attention. The other half was focused on Dad. She stared at him, and he stared at Bobby, and Bobby stared at the ground, then his feet, then the ground, then he looked at the lions again like he was giving serious thought to the safety the cage might provide him. It looked like he might go for it after all when Mom said, "I think that would be wonderful, Bobby."

"Oh shit," Abby said in a whisper. Then pulling her phone out of her pocket, and not looking at it, she added, "I'll be damned, it was stuck on vibrate and I missed a call. I'll be right back." And she wandered off with her phone, not dialing. I felt sorry for Bobby. Dad's eyes were yelling at him instead of Abby. Dad started to stand up, but I pulled on his arm and typed, "It's okay Dad. I don't want to go. I was only asking."

Dad looked down at me. His eyes stopped yelling. When he looked at me his eyes were sad and tired. The same eyes I remember from my childhood. The same eyes I always wish I could take away the sad from. He sighed, shook his head, and said, "No, your mother's right, and you're lying. I know you want to go, and you deserve to."

He leaned over and kissed the top of my head. Then he pointed at Bobby and said, "You, follow me. You listen to what I say. You do not speak until I say speak. You do not interrupt. You keep your ears open to every word I say. Am I clear?"

Bobby stared at Dad and didn't say anything. Bobby was used to Dad. He was scared of Dad. He looked like he might pee his pants at any second, but he didn't say anything. Dad nodded and said, "Good. Now speak, am I clear?"

"Yes sir," Bobby stammered and followed when Dad walked past him. Todd shouted to their backs, "Don't break his thumbs, Dad! We're having an Xbox tournament tonight!" He laughed as Dad walked away with Bobby right behind him.

Abby wandered back over and asked, "Papa Cooper's going to let you go?"

I said, "Yeah."

She smiled and hugged me. Mom laughed and said, "See, I knew it would be a good idea."

Abby whispered in my ear, "I promise I won't let you get lost in the fog. Not this time. I promise."

Chapter Twenty-three

It turned out Abby didn't have to worry about keeping her promise. Dad planned on taking care of that himself. My dad is weird, he's silly, he's funny, but he also is the quickest thinker I know. I'm sure the second he said no in front of the lions' cage at the zoo without turning around he already had the backup plan of going to prom as a chaperone ready. But instead, he let everybody think he was being a tough guy. He sure scared poor Bobby. When they got back from their walk Bobby wouldn't look at anybody, even Todd. He just looked at his feet the entire time we stayed at the zoo. On the way home Dad announced to everyone that he'd call the school first thing Monday and let them know he'd be going as a chaperone, which I guess is like a grown-up volunteer security person to make sure the kids all behave. Dad would be good at that. He is still very big and very strong, even though he says all the time how old he is and how he isn't what he used to be. He likes to say, "It's the miles not the years," but he doesn't really drive all that much so I'm not sure what he means. I still see him as this friendly giant that smiles at kids on the playground or at the store and juggles to make them laugh, but if you didn't know him I bet you'd be scared of him. Bobby has known my dad his whole life and he's still scared of him. It's funny because people are scared of Dad, but Abby is more likely to hit somebody who has made fun of me than Dad. Abby's a lot meaner than Dad is. So Dad as chaperone security would be a good thing, at least that's what I thought. I don't know why Mom and Abby glared at him when he said it.

Prom was a month away when we were at the zoo and Bobby said he'd take me. Mom and Abby were really excited over the next few weeks before prom, but Dad just looked sad and tired. I love Dad, but I didn't want to be sad and tired. I wanted to be happy like Mom and Abby, so I went with them to look at dresses. You have to wear fancy clothes to go to prom I guess. We went to dozens of stores at several different shopping malls and tried on dress after dress after dress. It was fun at first, but after so many stores, way more than five stores, it got to be boring. One dress looks like another after a while, only the colors change. But, Mom and Abby never seemed to get bored with it, so I tried to be excited for them.

The week before prom Abby was over at our house while Bobby and Todd were playing video games in the living room. Mom, Abby, and me were out in the kitchen trying to pick the restaurant we were going to go to before prom. The restaurant is supposed to be fancy like the clothes, so Mom and Abby were scrolling through their choices on Mom's computer and making *Ooo* and *Ahhh* noises over different menus. They had been looking at restaurants for hours when I typed, "Pizza?" into my talker, and Mom said, "No sweetie, prom isn't really a pizza kind of thing-"

"Wait Mrs. Cooper," Abby interrupted her. "Antonio's downtown has all kinds of specialty pizzas, look," and she turned the computer so Mom could see the menu. Mom said, "Ooo look, *pine nuts and caramelized onions with goat cheese pizza.* That sounds very nice."

Dad was drinking a cup of coffee and leaning back against the wall, looking between the living room and where we sat at the kitchen table. He snorted and dribbled a bit of coffee down his chin. Wiping it away he said, "Oh yeah, that sounds like something Megan would enjoy. Pine nuts are just what she's been missing all these years."

Mom glared over at Dad and said, "Don't be an ass, John."

He shook his head and smiled at her. Dad still had that tired look in his eyes, no matter how many cups of coffee he drank. I always thought coffee was supposed to wake you up, but Dad always looked tired. Maybe too much coffee can make you tired again? He put his mug down and poured some more from the pot into it. As he added sugar, he said, "Hey now, would an ass have the class to spring for his daughter to go to prom in a limo?"

"I thought Ryan was driving us?" Abby asked, glaring over at Dad and looking a lot like Mom when she did it. Dad laughed. Not the mean laugh. It wasn't his tired laugh either. I'd never heard him laugh that way before. I don't have the right words for it. It was a laugh that was too sad to be mean - if that makes sense? He said, "You can let whatever floppy-haired mimbo is taking you drive the two of you, Abs. But, I'm not letting him drive Megan. Jim owns his own plumbing business. He's got plenty set aside to help out. We both decided that Bobby is going to have enough to do keeping an eye on Megan, so we figured we'd split the bill on the limo and give the kid one less distraction."

"Not to mention constant adult supervision because of the limo driver," Abby said in her bitchy voice that she usually says is because of PMS – more silly initials for words. Dad shrugged his shoulders and said, "Call that a bonus. I relented on playing dinner chaperone too, if you remember. I was going to go to dinner with you. We had that very long 'discussion' about me being overprotective, but, I mean I still could go to dinner too if you'd rather I do that. I sure do love pine nuts!" Both Mom and Abby glared harder at Dad. He laughed and said, "This is a way to split the difference. You get to pretend you're all responsible adults out for a special dinner without me cramping your style with my overprotectiveness, and I still know there is a man - a man I happen to be paying good money to - there watching to make sure you don't do anything stupid. I call that a fair trade don't you, Bobby?" Dad looked into the living room where Bobby and Todd were still playing. Bobby didn't say anything. Dad nodded his head in approval and raised his eyebrows at Mom before he said, "Speak Bobby."

"Yes sir," Bobby said immediately after Dad spoke. "That sounds like a fair trade to me."

"See," Dad motioned toward Bobby with his coffee mug. Abby and Mom were both still glaring at him, their eyes looked mad and yelling, but Dad didn't seem to care at all. I wish I could ignore people's eyes like Dad does. He said, "You and your mimbo can either drive yourselves, probably in some beat-up piece of crap car, plus pay for gas, or you can ride in style. It's up to you."

"Fine," Abby said and stopped glaring. "Thanks Papa Cooper."

Dad nodded and added, "Hell, there should be enough room in there – it seats nine – you can ask that spoiled rich girl from the swim team if she wants to go too."

"Wendy?" Abby asked. "No, she's going with Hunter Jackson. He has a Mustang GT convertible. It's the whole reason she's going to prom with him. She's even spending the entire morning next Saturday at Vincent's Beauty Shop having her hair plated and braided to her head so if they ride with the top down it won't mess her hair up."

Dad nodded seriously, but his eyes went from tired to sparkling and happy as he said, "Alright, I'll be sure to file that away in my I don't give a shit drawer. But I'm warning you now that sucker is getting awfully full lately. I may just have to forget all about Wendy's convertible hair."

Todd started laughing in the living room and Mom chuckled a little, which is the most she laughs when Dad says something other people think is funny. Abby stuck her tongue out at Dad, but Dad winked and said over his shoulder, "You can laugh too, Bobby."

Bobby laughed along with Todd, and Dad raised his mug at Mom when she shook her head.

Chapter Twenty-four

Dinner was really nice. I had never been to Antonio's before so everything was new: the people, the tables with candles, the napkins that were cloth and not paper. The limo driver held the door for us to get out, a guy in a suit and tie held the restaurant door for us when we went in, and a woman in a fancy dress like Abby's and mine pulled out the chairs from our table for us to sit down. Both Bobby and Abby's date wore black suits. Abby called them tuxedoes, but Dad had called them penguin suits. I was a little worried that they made the clothes out of penguins and I was about to type that into my talker, but Dad shook his head and told me it was a joke, before I could type a single word. At the restaurant Bobby walked around the table and quickly wrapped up all the spoons in a napkin that he put on an empty chair. I smiled at him. Spoons hadn't bothered me for years, but he wasn't going to take any chances with the fog, or my dad too, I guess.

I could feel the fog pressing on me the entire time, from when we left the house in the long black car, and all the way through dinner. I wanted to be normal. I wanted to be like everybody else and have a good time … without hiding in the water. Just a chance to be like everybody else for one night, that's all I wanted, just one night, so I fought the fog with every bit of energy that I had. It couldn't even whisper. All it could do was press...

....

...But it still tried. The fog wanted me to embarrass myself at the nice restaurant, to show everybody there I didn't belong, that I shouldn't be out there with them. I fought back harder than I have in a long time. At dinner I ordered a margherita pizza, which I was worried that I wouldn't be allowed to have at first because I thought a margherita was a drink with alcohol. But when I typed it out Bobby said it was okay. It didn't have alcohol in it, just tomatoes and cheese like the menu said it did. He ordered it for me, so I didn't have to use my talker with the waiter. He wasn't embarrassed. I just think he wanted the waiter to think I was like everybody else without the fog. I think Bobby realized how important it was for me. I think he wanted to try and help. I typed, "Thank you Bobby," and smiled when the waiter left with our orders.

He smiled back. Abby was busy talking away to her date Ryan. He was not really listening to her. He kept watching me out of the corner of his eye and then looking around like he expected to find my dad hiding behind a potted plant or under a table, because when they met Dad had told him to follow him like he had with Bobby at the zoo. They walked around the neighborhood two times before Dad would let Ryan into the limo. Abby glared at Dad when he did it, folding her arms across her chest and growling quietly like I used to when I was mad. Dad just smiled at her. He even waved when they passed on the second lap.

When he brought Ryan back, Abby's date looked like he wanted to find a lion cage to hide in, but he climbed into the limo instead. Dad leaned on the open door and said, "Have a nice dinner you four. I'll see you all at the dance." He slipped the limo driver another twenty dollars and nodded his head in Ryan's direction where he sat against the far side door. We couldn't hear what they said, but the driver looked at Ryan, his eyes hidden behind mirror sunglasses and he nodded. Bobby laughed a little from where he was sitting next to me on the long bench seat as Ryan squirmed.

Every time at dinner that I used my talker Ryan would jump a little in his seat, making Abby frown. We went to the bathroom, to powder our noses, Abby said, but I had to pee. She peed too, so I don't know what noses and powder had to do with it, but when she was putting on more lipstick – I didn't use any because the fog wanted me to eat it – she said, "I may lose, Megan, I may lose royally, but I think tomorrow I'm going to have to try kicking your dad's ass."

I laughed and typed, "Ryan looks more scared than Bobby did."

"Yeah," Abby said, growling again. "That's because Bobby knows your dad, and knows he'd only hurt a fly if he absolutely had to. But Ryan just took a 'walk' with a six and a half foot tall three hundred pound stranger that probably used words like: maim, rip, crush, pulverize, and balls all in the same sentence."

When she touched up her eyeliner – I didn't use any because the brush coming so close to my eye almost had me run into the fog – she added, "Even after we drop you guys off back home there is no way I'm getting lucky tonight. All thanks to your dad."

She meant sex when she said lucky. Mom and Abby had both talked to me about sex. I thought I understood the how and the why, but I didn't want to sound stupid, so I didn't ask too many questions. I asked Dad once and all he said was a bad word followed by, "Never. End of story. Go talk to your mother." I guessed Dad didn't want to talk about being lucky.

Dinner was nice, even with Ryan jumping at every noise or word I typed. My pizza was okay. It wasn't great. It was kind of dry and didn't have enough cheese and sauce on it, but Abby said it was supposed to be gourmet, which I think means expensive.

The limo driver came into the restaurant because it was getting late, and he said we didn't want to get to prom too late. He didn't want us to miss out on the whole point of going out. Ryan jumped again when the driver nodded at him and Abby growled.

When we got to prom, they had it at the high school gym but they put up all kinds of decorations and flowers to make it look like it wasn't the gym, lots of kids were there already. No matter how many streamers and strobe lights they added it was still the gym. People were still dancing on the foul ball lines. They were dressed like we were, in fancy clothes, pretending to be adults, like the gym was pretending to be a prom. But a lot of kids were hugging and dancing like they were someplace else. They were willing to pretend that they hadn't run up and down the prom gym and played dodgeball or kickball just yesterday morning, so I figured maybe that was what it felt like to be normal – just pretend like you're something else, someone else, or someplace else than where you really were, and you'd be normal. The music was really loud. I was worried it was going to push the fog back in. The fog didn't want me to figure out how to be normal. I could even hear the smallest whisper from the fog over the music…

…*Too loud, Megan?*…

…No, it wasn't. I could handle it. I wanted to be like all the other kids in my class. If they all went to school like I did, and they went to prom, then I should too. No matter how loud it was. No matter how much of it was just pretending to be something else. I wanted to do it like everybody else did. Abby and Ryan started dancing right away, but Bobby and I walked around the big cluster of people hugging to the music. Some of the boys were standing along one wall talking and some of the girls were standing against a different wall talking too, with the hugging dancers in-between them. Bobby didn't say anything. He just walked next to me. I think he was nervous. I hadn't seen Dad yet, and I think Bobby was afraid he was going to jump out and say boo like we used to when Todd was little. To be fair to Bobby, Dad might do that – even at prom. When we had walked a few laps, one of the boys moved over toward us when we walked past their side of the prom gym. He had a friend right behind him and they both smelled like beer. The first boy laughed the mean-eyed laugh as he said, "Look it's Bobby McGregor the Masturbator and the water tard."

Bobby glared at him. He looked like he wanted to say something but was kind of scared to. I could tell the other boy was being mean not just because of the anger in his eyes, but because Bobby looked mad and scared. He didn't get the chance to say something though, even if he hadn't been scared. The boy's friend grabbed his shoulder and said, "Are you crazy? Haven't you seen that her dad's a chaperone?"

"So?" the boy said and he wobbled a little bit like he was dizzy. His friend said, "So, he's the big guy dressed in jeans and a tee-shirt. He's the only guy here not wearing a tux, man."

"So what?" the boy said. "What's he going to do?"

Bobby started laughing because Dad was walking up behind the two boys and they didn't see him. They were looking at Bobby and me. I smiled and waved. The boys turned as Dad said in his real deep whisper voice that sucks the air out of a room, "He might ask you real nice to please apologize to his daughter and his friend."

The boys looked up at him, but didn't say anything back. Dad leaned down a little; crouching so he could look in the mean boy's yelling eyes. Dad smiled a not smile and said, "Or, he might remind you that gosh it's prom night, and kids tend to do stupid things on prom night, don't they Bobby my boy?"

"Yes sir," Bobby said.

"Yeah," Dad agreed nodding his head. "They sure do. They get drunk and get in car accidents all the time, or try to do some other silly thing while under the influence that could wind up causing them lots and lots of pain. Pain that the coroner would rule as accidental – horrible and excruciating – but accidental, you know, just the kind of thing that happens on prom night, right?"

Both boys turned to Bobby and me and said, "We're sorry."

Dad looked at the boy's friend and said, "You didn't do anything wrong kid."

The boy's friend said, "No sir, but I figured why take a chance on prom night, right?"

"I like you," Dad said smiling, then putting a hand on each of their shoulders he steered them toward the wall where the girls were standing. I heard him saying, "Now boys how about you go ask your dates to dance, huh?" as they walked away.

Bobby watched them go, and he said, "I wish my dad was like your dad."

I typed, "My dad's weird."

"Yeah," Bobby agreed, "but it's a good weird. My dad's a big fat coward who doesn't have the balls to say anything to anybody … just like me. He lets the world walk all over him and eats when he's upset."

I typed, "My dad eats like that too."

"Yeah," Bobby said, "but your dad isn't five foot four and round like a beach ball."

"Beach ball weird is okay too," I typed. "Everybody is weird, Bobby."

169

"Not everybody gets made fun of, Megan," Bobby said and looked at the prom gym floor. I typed, "So what? Weird is weird, some people need to make other people feel bad, so they can feel good. I think that's weird. It's all weird to me, Bobby. I don't know what's real sometimes and what isn't. Everybody is weird."

I grabbed his hand and stormed off toward the dancing, hugging bodies. Bobby whined, "Oh God, Megan no! I don't know how to dance. I'll look like an idiot and on Monday they'll all call me a new stupid name."

I stopped, pointed toward all the decorations that were disguising the gym, making it a prom, and typed, "So what? I don't know how to dance either. We're in the gym, pretending it's a dance floor. Isn't that weird? They already call us both names. What's one more? Let's have fun. Let's pretend we know how to dance. That's all everybody else is doing – just pretending."

Bobby smiled and nodded. We pushed our way into the hugging, swaying bodies and learned how to dance, or at least pretended to. Two weird people hugging in a group of weird people, dancing and pretending they were not in their high school gym, pretending that they weren't weird too, that dressing up in fancy clothes to hug in your high school gym covered in streamers and playing loud music was normal. For a few hours I was weird like everybody else without the fog, instead of being weird because of the fog.

Part III:
Adulthood

Chapter Twenty-five

Today was my thirty second birthday. I had to work on my birthday, but I didn't mind. I love my job and all my friends at work had a birthday party for me. They ordered pizza and had a cake on our lunch break; we all had a really good time. We even let a few of the bears have the leftover slices, but don't tell anybody that. I wasn't supposed to tell people we did that because they even put up signs saying *please don't feed the animals*, so it looks bad if we do it. But the bears love pizza and other junk food. Please don't go to your zoo and feed the bears just because I told you we feed ours. If they get too much junk food they'll get sick, but every now and then the keepers at our zoo say it's okay for them to have a little human food. The problem is when people give them junk food every day when they visit. A few slices of cold pepperoni pizza on my birthday weren't going to hurt them. I wanted them to celebrate with me. I love all of the animals at my zoo … it's not really my zoo, but I've gone there since I was a little girl, and now that I work there, and have been working there for years and years since high school, it feels like it's my zoo.

I wanted to give a few slices to the lions. They still make me sad. They are different lions than when I was a kid, but they still pace and it still makes me sad. Their keeper said they probably wouldn't like the pizza, but she let me feed them their big hunks of meat this morning so they could celebrate my birthday with me. It didn't seem to make them any happier or sadder. They just ate what I fed them and then paced their cage.

I didn't let the sad lions make me sad. I never do, even though I visit them every day I work. My job is to take people's tickets and stamp their hands. I can say, "Tick-ets," "Thank you," "En-joy," and a few other words so people don't think there is something wrong with me. The fog is still there, sticking the words in my throat, gaging me so I can't talk like other adults. But, I can do my job without using a talker, and that really makes the fog mad ... and I don't care. I love my job. My zoo has other workers that might have the fog, or something else that makes them different. The boss gives us jobs like taking tickets, cleaning up the trash, and other simple tasks. I could do more, but, like most people, my boss worries about the fog sweeping in while I'm at work and causing problems. He's a nice guy, but he doesn't want me feeding the lions without one of the animal keepers there. He probably thinks the fog will make me wrestle with the lions or some other silly thing that a person without the fog would never do. I wouldn't do it even with the fog (that's not crazy, that's stupid), but that doesn't keep my boss from worrying. So, I take people's tickets and let them into the zoo. It's fun because I get to see all the happy little kids on their way in. I try not to look at the ones that scream on the way out. Some scream and yell on the way in too, but I can never tell if that's just a kid being a kid or if they might have some kind of the fog bothering them too, so I just smile and say, "En-joy."

I take the bus to work hours before my shift starts and the zoo opens. Some days I get to help feed the animals, but most times I just enjoy sitting and watching the animals while the zoo is quiet. I pick a different animal to watch every morning. I always hope the lions will be happy, but their eyes tell me they're sad. The fish seem happy. They float in their giant fish tank, going about their fish days eating and swimming. The fish don't seem to notice or care that they're stuck in a box and people watch them all day, pointing, laughing, and saying things they don't understand. Even when somebody comes in to watch the fish and their eyes aren't happy, the fish don't notice or don't care. I think the fish have the best attitude of all the animals. The bears have slow sad eyes the longer they are in their zoo cages. Look at a bear that's been in a zoo its whole life. If it's been there thirty years or more you will never see slower eyes. They look as if they've not only forgotten what it means to be a bear, but their eyes look like they don't even know they are a bear. Not the fish, the fish don't care. The fish don't forget that they're fish. The fish just swim.

I took the bus home after my shift was over. My friends at work told me to have a happy birthday again as I left even though they'd already told me lots of times. They're nice people. I don't work with many mean-eyed people. There are a few sad, tired-eyed workers, but most are happy. Most of them like their jobs too. I think it helps if you like your job. Go someplace where people don't like their job, like the supermarket, and look at those people's eyes. Most of the time they look like the bears that have always lived in the zoo, like they don't know they are people anymore – their eyes aren't sad, mad, yelling, mean, or screaming. No, their eyes are blank. It scares me because I don't know if that's how they really are, or if that's the fog telling me that their eyes are blank. The fog isn't better or worse after so many years of having it as my constant companion. It's always back there whispering, mocking, and hurting me.

I ride the bus because of the fog. I don't really want to drive, but it's unfair that the fog keeps me from driving and it isn't because I just don't want to. The bus stops right by the zoo and there are also stops by the grocery store and at the end of the block near my apartment. It's what they call an assisted living apartment. I have my own place: living room, kitchen, bathroom, bedroom, and really tiny nook for a table, but there are people there to help me if I need it. Dad didn't want me to move out, but when Todd went away to college I wanted to be out on my own. I figured if Todd was so much younger than me and he could live on his own it was time I did, too. So, Dad and my social worker (she's a real nice lady named Betty) helped me find a place to live.

They help take care of my paychecks and banking and stuff – I'm not very good with remembering to pay the rent and when to pick up my medications, so either Betty, one of the people that work at my assisted living apartment building, or Dad, help me with those things. But, other than things like that, I get myself to work, and go to doctors' appointments, and shop for food, and stuff.

I have dinner with Mom and Dad three, four, or five – yes, five – times a week. Sometimes Todd comes over with his girlfriend, and other times he'll stop by the zoo to take me out for lunch. I like that. It makes me feel like a regular person to go out for lunch on my break. Todd works at a business near the zoo. He sells something, or sues people, or writes policies, or something like that. I can never remember exactly what it is he does. I know he works during the day in an office, and he wears lots of ties and jackets. He also swings by sometimes after work to make sure I don't need anything. I don't and I tell him I don't, but he still checks on me. It's sweet, but annoying. My apartment is only a short walk from Mom and Dad's house. That was one of the things Dad insisted on when he and Betty were looking for a place for me to live – it had to be close enough I could walk home if the fog ever freaked me out so much that I got lost. So, even if I needed something I wouldn't bother Todd, I'd just go see Dad.

The Fog Within

Mom and Dad are supposed to pick me up for my birthday dinner, but I got home early enough that I had to wait. I don't mind. It's funny how when I was a little girl waiting used to drive the fog wild, but if I'm home and waiting, without grown-up rules causing the waiting, the fog just keeps at its normal whisper instead of screaming at me to do something. When I get bored waiting, I do something like feed my fish. I have lots of different fish in my tank. Not as neat as the ones at the zoo, but I like them. Every now and then one dies, and I have to flush it down the toilet. I don't like it when the fish die. Their eyes go from being there, being a fish, being happy to white glazed-over and blank. I scoop them out when they die. I close my eyes once I have the dead fish in my little green net, so I don't have to see the fish that isn't a fish anymore, and walk carefully to the bathroom to flush it.

After I fed them and made sure there weren't any dead ones, I changed out of my work clothes and took a quick shower – which for me can still be a long time – I get lost in the water. A shower isn't as good as swimming, but I only go to the pool a few days a week now that I have a job and fish to look after. I still go, but not as often as I'd like, so letting the water from the shower pour over me gives me a chance to quiet the fog completely. When the hot water splashes against my skin all I am is water … no Megan, no yelling eyes, no sad eyes, no fog, no whispering, and no anything but warm water pounding on my face, arms, and chest. We have a big water heater in my apartment building … but sometimes one of the workers has to come ask me if I could take shorter showers because the other residents are complaining that there isn't any hot water. I try, but sometimes it's just too nice to disappear in the water that I forget and I'm in there for hours.

I remembered to keep the shower short, so I was ready when Mom and Dad showed up to take me out for dinner. Dad brought me a present and I typed, "Dad, I'm too old for presents."

He laughed and said, "Fine, I'll just take it back if you don't want it." He started to walk back toward the door, but I heard the box meow. I typed, "Really? I can have a cat?" I'd been trying for years to convince Mom and Dad that I could have a cat - that I could take care of something bigger than a fish. There were rules about pets at my apartment building, a long silly list of approved and unapproved, but what it really meant was just no dogs, because dogs bark and can annoy your neighbors. Cats and fish and hamsters and other quiet animals were okay. I had wanted a cat ever since I realized I could have one. Dad laughed and handed me back the present. I opened it and a tiny all black face with green eyes blinked at me from the box. Its eyes were scared, but curious, eyes that wanted to be happy, but were too scared to be until it knew it was safe. I reached in and petted its head. The kitten flinched back for a second, but when it

179

realized I wanted it to be happy not scared, that I wanted to take care of it, it purred and started rubbing its tiny head against my hand. I sat down on my couch and let the kitten climb out of the box and curl up in my lap. I typed, "Thanks Mom, thanks Dad!"

Mom smiled and sat down next to me. Dad said, "I'll go get the rest of the supplies: litter box, food, and stuff." He popped his head back in the door and asked, "Should I just order some pizza, Megan? I figure you don't want to leave your new friend alone right away."

I typed around the kitten trying to make my fingers pet it, "Had pizza for lunch. Mexican?"

Dad laughed and shrugged, saying, "It's your birthday, kiddo. You can have whatever you want. I'll give Todd a call and tell him we're staying in. He'll probably want to stop over, too."

I didn't even realize Dad had left when the door shut behind him. I had my own kitten. I was so excited. Mom petted the tiny black head as it walked back and forth on my couch between us. She asked, "So honey, what are you going to name him?"

I didn't know. I never thought I'd be allowed a cat, so I'd never thought of names. But looking at the tiny black face, I realized I didn't know what to name him. When you name something it has that name forever, right? So it's pretty important to think about it. I typed, "Don't know, Mom. I have to think about it. Names are important. I need to find out who he is first."

Chapter Twenty-six

The next morning the cat woke me up before my alarm. I'd heard from lots of people with cats that they do that. I didn't mind though; he was curled up in bed with me and his tail tickled my nose. It slowly woke me up instead of startling me like my alarm clock does. Before I went to bed last night, I had shown him the fish tank and told him the fish were his friends, not food. I don't think he understood, but the tank is one of those built-in ones that is part of my desk. My new cat would have to have thumbs and fingers and super kitty strength to be able to get to my fish, so I wasn't worried about him going fishing after I fell asleep. His tiny black tail kept flicking under my nose, keeping me awake. I looked over at my clock and saw I didn't have to get out of bed for another half an hour, so I lay there and let the cat's tail tickle me. It wasn't annoying and I liked how he purred when he did it. His voice sounded like a soft motor where he was curled up against my shoulder, sharing my pillow.

Todd had come over with his girlfriend Susie last night and they had dinner with us at my apartment. It was nice, a little cramped with five people and a cat, but still nice. It made me feel like a real person, like a person without the fog, like a person on TV that had their own place that people stopped by to say hi and have dinner. It's small things like that that help cut through the fog, help make me keep going when things seem too dark, too hazy, too foggy. As we ate dinner, tacos are my favorite food right behind pizza, everybody had all kinds of suggestions for names for my new cat, but I kept typing, "No, I don't know who he is yet."

How do you name something? I tried naming my fish, but that seemed silly. It's not like they could hear my talker through the tank and come swimming over if I typed, "Flip and Goldie, come!"

So I wanted to take my time with the cat. I didn't want to name him something simple like Blackie or Smokey, which were some of my family's suggestions. If I was going to be typing his name over and over - or trying to say it aloud if we were alone in my apartment and I wasn't worried about sounding stupid if it didn't come out right - then I wanted it to be something that made sense for him. Dad said I should name him Mooch because he kept trying to get Dad to give him some of his taco meat instead of the cat food Mom and Dad had bought for him. Mom said it was only because the cat could tell Dad was a pushover. She was right too, because Dad kept giving him taco meat even though he complained about it. He'd say, "There, enjoy it fuzzball, because that's your last piece. You aren't getting anymore from me!" But, a minute later the cat went right back to him, and after complaining about it, Dad gave the cat more.

183

The Fog Within

I didn't want to get out of bed, but I had to go to work. I wanted to go to work, because I love my job … but, I also didn't want to leave my new cat all by himself. I was worried. I didn't want him to be scared, all alone in a new place. I didn't want him to get hurt with so many dangers in my apartment. The fog started to whisper…

…If you leave he will get hurt, Megan. You'll come home from work and find him like the fish. His happy green eyes will be glazed-over and gone. If you leave the cat will die, and nobody will ever trust you again…

…I slipped out of bed as quietly as I could, because I didn't want to wake him up. I even turned my alarm off so it wouldn't wake him. I wandered around my apartment to make sure it was safe. I left out two bowls of food and two bowls of water. I wanted to leave the toilet seat up, so if he got really thirsty he could get a drink from there. But I was scared he might fall in and drown, so I figured two bowls of water had to be good enough. A cat couldn't die of thirst during my six hour shift, right? I put his extra bag of kitty litter on top of the closed toilet seat so he couldn't open the lid, fall in, and drown … but then I got worried that the bag would fall off the toilet and crush him, so I took it off and hoped he wouldn't be able to open the seat on his own. Then I remembered to just shut the door to the bathroom and I wouldn't have to worry about it at all. I had his litter box in my small utility closet.

184

There was nothing in there that could hurt him, but I checked several times and turned the light on and off half a dozen times before I decided it was really safe. I double checked that all my windows were locked so he couldn't get out and nobody could get in to steal him either. By the time I was done making sure my apartment was safe for my cat I was running late. I locked and unlocked my front door five times before I was confident that it had latched, and I almost missed my bus.

The entire ride to work the fog kept whispering…

…The cat isn't going to be alive when you get home, Megan. Everybody will be disappointed in you, because you couldn't take care of a tiny kitten. You can't take care of yourself, Megan; you have no business taking care of a sweet and innocent kitten…

…I did my best to ignore the fog. I was glad to see my stop though. Once I was at work I could think about that instead. I could forget about my cat and forget about worrying if he was safe or scared without me there. I was still early enough that I stopped and watched the lions for a few minutes. They were eating their breakfast, which is kind of gross to see, but it's one of the few times they look happy … sort of. You can still see the sadness in their eyes though. You can see that they are upset because they didn't hunt and kill their breakfast themselves. They want to be free and do things like

185

they are supposed to, like wild lions, but even if they didn't catch their breakfast it's still food, so maybe they just pretend they're happy like everybody else does. Pretend they are real lions, and pretend that the world is what they want it to be, even if it's just while they eat their breakfast.

When I open my ticket booth there is a short line already, so I just take people's money, tear their tickets, stamp their hands, and say, "En-joy," as quick as I can to catch up. It wasn't a long line or anything, but I remember how much the fog hated for me to wait when I was little, and in case there is somebody in line with their own version of the fog I don't want to keep them waiting just because I stopped to watch the lions pretend to be real lions. While I stamp an older couple's hands, I notice my phone vibrate. I tell the older couple, "Thank you, en-joy," and then look at my phone since the line is finally empty.

It's Abby. She sent, "So sorry I missed it yesterday, honey. Happy birthday a day late! Ethan had a soccer game and I had to take some work home. By the time I got him in bed I pretty much passed out myself, sorry. I hope you had a good day."

I sent back, "I did. Thanks, Abby. Mom and Dad got me a cat!"

I hadn't seen Abby in years. She got her wish and moved away for college, too far away, all the way to the other side of the country. I've seen her twice since we graduated high school. It makes me sad. I miss her. We used to have so much fun together. She came back that first Christmas and she was all talk - nonstop for most of her visit - about how much she loved it out on the coast, and how she was seeing this guy, and they were both business majors, and all kinds of stuff they had in common. She was very excited, so I was excited for her. I had started working at the zoo by then so I told her about that … when she had to pause to breathe. But, when she went back out to school after that break she didn't come home for years and years.

We sent each other messages and emails as often as we thought about it. Which as the years went by became less and less often. No matter how many messages I sent, hinting that maybe she'd come home for Christmas or something, she didn't. She finished school and started working someplace out there, doing something in an office, or something like Todd does. I don't know. I can never remember the different office jobs and what people do at them, suing people, writing policies, or filing reports of some kind. I hated writing reports in school. I can't imagine how boring it must be to write reports as a job. After college she got pregnant with some guy's baby, but the guy was a loser Abby said, so she left him. Dad told me he thinks it was the other way around, but I'm not supposed to tell Abby that. She had a little boy that she named Ethan and she brought him home once when he was two. He looked so much like Todd did at that age I wanted to call him Tahbey, but I said, "Hi E-than."

He called me Aunt Megan. I smiled and used my talker to type a longer hello. Ethan wasn't scared of my talker. He thought it was neat and wanted to play with it.

Abby sends me pictures of Ethan and her, when she remembers, and he's growing up fast. I miss them, even though I only met Ethan once. But ... I really miss Abby. She got her wish. She's happy. She's someplace where she met all new people and someplace her mom isn't. So, I'm happy for her, but I still miss her. I wish she would come home more often.

My phone vibrated again (my boss lets me have it out, but it has to be on vibrate, and I can't ignore the customers to send a message). Abby had sent, "That's great, Megan! What does it look like and what are you going to name it?"

I typed back, "He's all black with happy green eyes, but I haven't named him yet. I want to get to know him better. I want to find out what his name is, not just give him one."

I took a few more tickets and waved to a little girl who was carrying a small stuffed tiger in with her. Her mom was pulling her in a wagon. The little girl waved and growled, showing me her tiger. I smiled and growled back. The girl's mom was talking into her phone and kept on walking after I stamped her hand. The girl waved to me as her mom pulled her away, still talking. My phone vibrated. Abby had sent, "That sounds brilliant, Megan! Only you would want to figure out the cat's name and not just give him one. I got to run. I love you, miss you, and happy birthday again. Sorry I was late."

I typed back, "Thanks. I miss and love you too."

That's about how much contact we have anymore. It makes me sad. We used to be so close, but now we just send each other messages or emails every couple of months, and go about our separate lives. Abby will always be special to me. She was the first person to be my friend and not because she was family, or she was a teacher or therapist, but because she wanted to be my friend. I've had more friends since, but they'll never be as important to me as Abby. I wish I could drive so I could go see her and Ethan. I don't think I'd want to be in a car that long though. Sometimes when the bus has to make more stops because it's busy, the fog starts to push in harder, and that's just a few extra minutes on a bus. I can't imagine hour after hour in a car. No, I wish Abby would come home more often, and bring Ethan with her ... but I bet she doesn't even think of where I live as home anymore. It's home for me, but home for Abby is thousands of miles away.

It was a slow afternoon at the zoo. Weekdays are more likely to be slow, but that's why my boss has me work during the week most times. He doesn't make me work Saturdays – the busiest day of the week – because he worries the fog might make me get flustered and I might freak out and scare the visitors. It's kind of nice to not work Saturdays. None of my other friends at work seem to mind that I don't work the weekend. I do work two Sundays a month, so it's not like I get the whole weekend off. They all know about the fog. They all call it different things just like everyone always has: Megan's special, Megan's autistic, Megan's schizo-fran-something, Megan's got problems, Megan has issues, and all kinds of other things. They know, but they don't know. They only know what they hear from people on TV, or in movies, and stuff like that. They don't know what the fog is really like.

After the morning gate opening rush and the few people that sleep-in and show up later, I don't have much to do until my lunch break. It's hard to wait sometimes just as it is, but with the thought of my new kitten sitting at home all alone, probably scared and wondering where I was, the fog kept whispering…

…He's dead, Megan. Your cat is dead, just like the fish – glazed-eyed and gone…

…No, I knew my cat my fine. There was no reason or way he could have been hurt. Everything was alright. I made sure the apartment was safe…

190

...Fine, maybe not dead, but scared for sure. Scared and meowing. He's yelling his little head off at the door. He's hoping you'll come in any second and play with him. He's all alone, Megan, locked in his room just like you were at night and hoping Mommy will come in any second and ask you to help her work. He's all alone, Megan, and he's scared...

... "Miss, excuse me miss. Hello, anybody home?" A woman's voice snapped me out of the fog. She was glaring at me with annoyed, impatient eyes as she said, "Well it's about time. I've been standing here forever. What are they even paying you for? I need three tickets – one adult and two children."

I gave her the tickets and stamped her and her kids' hands. She stormed off into the zoo still complaining that I'd made her wait. There was nobody behind her in line, and when I glanced at the clock on my phone no more than a few minutes had passed since I'd last looked. She couldn't have been waiting for more than a minute - probably a lot less. But that didn't stop her from being mean and yelling at me with her eyes. The fog hides things from me. I don't see the world like everybody else. I know that, but I'll never understand why so many people think the world is there to do what they want, when they want it, and they're mean to anybody who they think isn't doing things exactly as they should. A minute isn't that long of time. It isn't any reason to be rude and mean to somebody, is it? I see it all the time

through the fog – people yelling at each other with
their eyes and mouths … just because of one minute.
I don't think I'll ever understand that.

Chapter Twenty-seven

When my shift was over I wanted to rush back home to check on my cat and make sure he was safe. To make sure that he wasn't scared, or frightened, or hurt, or dead. I wanted to run through the zoo to my locker, run as fast as I could. I wanted to run from the zoo after I put my coat on, run as fast as I could. I wanted to run to the bus stop, run as fast as I could. Of course you can't do that. You can't run in public as fast as you can because people will think that there is something wrong with you. They will think some kind of fog is driving you on if you run down the streets, or through a zoo, store, or park as fast as you can in your regular work clothes. It's only okay to run in public if you're a kid, or if you're running in one of the approved places like a track. Even then you have to do it in the approved clothes and at the proper arms pumping with rhythm pace. If you race out of your job in jeans and a regular jacket, arms flying everywhere as you try to run as fast as you can … somebody is going to stop you to see if you need help, or they'll stop you because they think you've done something wrong. Those are just the rules; don't run unless it's where and how everybody has agreed to run.

I walked really, really, really fast past the lions and all the other animals I normally stay after work to watch. I walked really, really, really fast down to the bus stop. And if you could wait fast, then I waited fast too. I waited until the bus stopped then I raced onto it and waited fast some more. I waited and watched the houses and buildings go by out the window. They blurred because the fog was pressing in on me. One big blur out the window, then a certain house or building would stick out, solid and real against the blur. The houses and buildings that stuck out looked scared and sad like I was sure my cat was at home. The sad house faces mocked me as the bus rode past really, really, really slow.

I walked really fast off the bus as soon as it stopped. I mean really fast. By that time I was so close to home I let the fog push me over and I started to run. I didn't care if somebody tried to stop me because I wasn't wearing approved running clothes or running in an approved way. I was so close to home I would just run past them if they tried. I raced down my sidewalk as the fog whispered...

...*Scared, scared, scared, Megan. Happy green-eyed kitten is scared and sad. He's all alone and scared because he doesn't understand the world outside of his cage. You know what that's like. Run, run, run, Megan!*...

...I raced up the steps and fumbled with my keys until I had the right one out and I unlocked the door. The fog lied. The fog almost always lies. My cat wasn't sitting in front of the door crying like the fog had me convinced that he would be. I didn't see him in the kitchen or the living room. I checked the stove and the refrigerator because I was worried he may have somehow opened and climbed in one of those then gotten stuck, but he wasn't in either one. I was worried that he'd gotten out somehow and had run away, maybe through a window or if one of the workers here came in to check and see if everything was okay. Maybe Betty my social worker had come over to make sure I'd been taking all my new pills, old pills, red pills, blue pills and my kitten ran away when she wasn't looking. But I found him on my bed, pretty much in the same place I had left him. He lifted his head up when I walked into the room. His eyes were still happy and green, not sad or scared at all. He rolled over onto his back and wanted me to scratch his stomach. I laughed - all that worry and he was fine. My cat liked his cage. He didn't want out like the lions. He didn't want to be free. He wanted to stay hidden and tucked away. He didn't know what was outside the walls of his cage, and he didn't want to know. He was happy with the space he had. He was happy being what he was. He didn't want anything else. He didn't pace and pretend he was free. The fog didn't have anything to say to that. It was nice.

I scooped my tiny black kitten up and carried him into the kitchen with me. He purred and purred while I carried him around. I had some leftovers from last night that I was going to heat up for dinner, so I put the food in the oven and carried my cat out to the couch. I placed him down on a pillow and he kept purring. I went over to feed my fish and he hopped down to follow me and rubbed against my legs the entire time. All my fish were there with bright fish eyes shining, swimming, floating, moving, and just happy to be fish.

I went back to the couch and my cat followed me. He jumped up onto my lap so I'd pet him. I did and while I rubbed at the fur behind his ears with one hand I typed into my talker with the other. "You know cat, you're really lucky. The fish are lucky too, but they don't even know to be happy about it, they just are. But you cat, you don't care that you are missing things, that the world outside is passing you by and other cats are doing other things you'll never do. You're happy just being where you are."

My cat purred as I typed to him. His eyes were mostly closed as I scratched at the back of his head. I realized if he was so happy with life, then that should be his name. I typed, "Happy, that's who you are. Okay cat? Your name is Happy."

His only response was to purr louder and roll over so I could scratch his stomach again. I wished that Abby could meet my cat Happy. I bet Ethan would like Happy, too. I wished my friend would come home. I wished I could be happy like Happy, that I could see the fog as the cage it was and not care. I wished for a lot of things while I sat there petting my new cat Happy. The worst part was that some of those whishes did come true, but if I had known what was going to happen the next day to make those wishes come true (even without a stupid star falling, no spent dandelions to blow on, and no wishing wells to drop quarters down) I know I would have had a different wish. A wish that would have made all the others seem silly and childish by comparison.

Chapter Twenty-eight

Happy woke me up again the next morning with his tail. It was even closer to when I had to get up than the day before, so I got out of bed and let Happy curl back up with my pillow after I turned my alarm clock off. I wasn't as worried about Happy as I was the day before. I knew he was going to be fine if I left everything the way it was: two bowls of food, two bowls of water, and the bathroom door shut. He hadn't even finished one bowl of either food or water yesterday, so I figured it'd be better for him to have too much than too little. The only thing I did out of habit was I locked and unlocked the door five times before I was willing believe it was locked, then I could safely leave for work.

I was early for my shift because I hadn't had to Happy-proof my apartment like yesterday, so I had plenty of time to pick an animal and watch the keepers feed them before the people started to arrive and the zoo opened. I decided it felt like an aquarium morning. I wanted to be happy like my cat and not sad like the lions. The fish should be able to make me happy. The huge floor to ceiling fish tank and all the colorful fish that floated, swam, and darted about always made me smile. I wondered if Happy was happy enough for me to go to the pool tomorrow on my day off. Watching the fish made me want to swim again. I didn't need the water to hide from the fog, it still helped to quiet the fog, but I could swim and just enjoy the motion, enjoy the moment, be like my cat Happy and just enjoy my cage.

I started my shift and let people into the zoo. I tried to be like Happy as I told them, "Thank you," and "En-joy," most of the people said thank you back, but some ignored me. That happens all the time. People don't look at or talk to the person who sits behind a counter. I don't know if they do it on purpose because I take their money, give them a ticket instead, and they don't feel that's an even trade or what. Maybe they just don't want to see other people in their cage while they are out of theirs. I don't think of my job as a cage, but some people might see my small booth as one. Maybe they don't want to look at me in my cage and say thank you back while they're free and outside. Maybe that doesn't seem fair to them. Maybe it makes them feel guilty that they're free and I'm in a cage. Maybe that makes them feel like I do when I look at the lions.

I hadn't been working for more than an hour or two when my boss Sam walked up to my ticket booth. He wears a jacket and tie all the time like Todd does. Ties don't look comfortable to me. Why would anybody want to wear a colored rope around their neck? It looks like a leash on a dog and the owner is just letting it dangle there instead of pulling on it. He was smiling, even though his tie looked too tight, but his eyes were sad and scared. I was worried about his eyes because Sam usually has nervous, but happy eyes. He likes animals a lot just like I do, so he enjoys his job. His voice kind of cracked when he said, "Megan, your brother's here to take you to lunch. I'll go ahead and cover the ticket window for you."

I typed, "Early? I just started. Lunch isn't for another two hours."

He looked sadder still, but he smiled and tried to look happy. His eyes couldn't manage it. Everybody knows I take my job seriously. I like letting people into the zoo, so when most people would jump at the chance for an early break, I get defensive. I don't want somebody else doing *my* job for me. I can handle my job. I'm crazy not stupid. Sam said, "I know it's early, Megan ... but this is a special occasion. He's waiting for you back in the employees' lounge."

I still didn't understand and I was getting more suspicious while Sam stammered. I typed, "But lunch is always the same time, even on my birthday."

He looked like he wanted to run away, like I had said something to scare him, or make him sad, and he didn't want to talk to me anymore. He just wanted me to go to lunch with my brother and stop asking him questions. I could see it all in his eyes, but he didn't say anything like that, even if his eyes wanted him to. He said, "It's okay, Megan. Todd will tell you what's going on when you go see him."

A mom and her kids were walking up to my ticket booth and my boss never looked so happy to have some customers. To me he said, "Go on, Megan," then turning away like I'd already gone, he said to the mom, "Hello, how many?"

I left my booth and walked back through the zoo offices to the employee lounge. It isn't far from my ticket booth. I could see Todd sitting in one of the soft lounge chairs with his back to the door, so he didn't notice me standing in the doorway. He had his face buried in his hands and he was breathing slowly in and out like some people do when they're trying to relax. I thought if he was trying to relax it might be fun to tease him like Dad and I used to when he was little. We'd jump out from behind a closed door and scare him. We'd say, "Boo Tahbey!" And he'd jump, then laugh and giggle until we did it again.

I snuck up behind Todd and pushed on his shoulder as I said, "Boo Tahbey!"

He jumped and I laughed, but when Todd turned around he wasn't laughing. He looked really sad and his eyes were red and wet like he had been crying. I typed, "Sorry Todd, I didn't mean to scare you so bad. I didn't know you'd cry. You always liked it when you were little."

Todd smiled, but he still didn't laugh. He said, "No sis, it isn't that."

The Fog Within

I typed, "What's wrong? My boss acted weird and wouldn't tell me why you were here early."

Todd's eyes got wetter and redder like he was going to start crying. He said, "It's Dad, Megan. He … he had a massive heart attack last night. I've … oh God, Megan, I've been at the hospital all night with Mom. Susie's there with her now. The doctors are saying they don't expect him to make it through the day, so I wanted to come down here and get you … you know, so you could see him … before … before," and then Todd did start crying.

It felt like someone had pulled my stomach up through my mouth. I wanted to vomit, but kept it down out of habit. I hoped more than anything I had ever hoped or dreamed or wished for that the fog had slipped up on me and I hadn't noticed – that Todd wasn't really there and that he hadn't really just told me that my dad was about to die. I couldn't even make myself use my talker. I stood there searching for signs that the fog was playing a mean trick on me. I looked for something not right, like a different colored chair, or Todd changing into somebody else, or anything, something, anything that would mean it was the fog being mean to me and that it wasn't real. Nothing, there was nothing out of place. Todd was real. He was still crying. The fog wouldn't even whisper to me. It was quieter than it had ever been in my life, even when I was swimming.

Todd stopped crying and grabbed my hand. He led me through the zoo offices and I let him. I stared off past him, watching what we were doing like it were a bad late-night movie on TV, all out of focus and fuzzy. I don't remember getting into Todd's car or the ride over to the hospital. I don't think it was the fog stealing time from me. I think my mind couldn't wrap around the idea of Dad dying, of Dad turning into a glazed-eyed fish. His eyes had always been tired and sad, but there was a spark there that I thought would never go out. It couldn't go out. It wasn't fair. That spark couldn't go out and leave me alone. That spark was always supposed to be there. Dad promised me he'd always be there. The fog did chime in then…

…Yes it can, Megan. You know it can. You've always known it could and that it would. You've known all those times he was there for you that at some point he wouldn't be. You knew the spark could go out. You knew that it would, but you never wanted to think about it. It's too late now, Megan. The spark is fading and soon it will be gone…

…Todd opened the car door for me and leaned in. I was still staring straight ahead. I didn't turn to look at him. He asked, "Are you okay, sis? You haven't said anything since we left."

I pulled out my talker and typed, "Are you okay, Tahbey?"

The Fog Within

He shook his head and said, "No, you're right, good point." He pulled on my arm to help me out of the car and I let him. When I was out and on my feet I hugged him hard. He stumbled back a step, then he hugged me hard back and I could feel him crying again. My eyes wouldn't let me cry. The fog wouldn't let me cry. Eyes are so powerful. They can do so much to a person. They can lie or tell the truth. They can help or they can hurt. My eyes refused to cry until it was over. I would not cry, because that would be admitting that the spark was going to go out. I wouldn't believe it until I saw it. Doctors don't know everything. They don't know about the fog. They can call it all kinds of smart doctor names, but have they figured out how to get rid of the fog? No they haven't, and they probably never will, or if they do some new and improved fog will just sweep in and they'll be stumped all over again. There always was and always will be a fog for some people. Doctors don't know that, so they don't know everything. Maybe my dad would be fine. Maybe the doctors were wrong. I walked into the hospital holding my younger brother's hand and I could hear the fog laughing at me.

Chapter Twenty-nine

The fog can say what it likes, but I never thought I'd see Dad – my daddy the friendly giant – looking so weak and small. There were all kinds of monitors around him beeping and making strange noises. He lay in the middle of a big bed with tubes and wires running out from him, under the blankets and up from his robe, to the monitors and computers and machines. The tubes were in his hand, under his nose, and wires were attached to his chest. He looked pale and sick…

…Just like a glazed-eyed fish, Megan…

…Mom got up real fast from a chair when she saw me and hugged me harder than Todd had. I hugged her hard back. Todd went over and sat down next to Susie, his girlfriend, and she rubbed his neck while he put his face back in his hands. Mom wouldn't stop hugging me. She held on like she was afraid something was going to happen to me too. That if she hugged me hard enough and long enough, I'd be safe.

After a while she stopped hugging me, but she held my hand. She didn't want to let go and I didn't want her to. She led me over to another chair that one of the nurses had brought in for me. The small room was very crowded with four chairs, the monitors, and Dad's bed all squeezed into it, and we all sat watching the biggest man we knew slowly get smaller and smaller. I don't know if the others saw it like I did. I doubt it. The fog makes things different. I think they just watched Dad's body weaken and fail. But with the fog I saw the most important person to me slowly shrink and start to fade away. There was no failing or weakening. He was getting smaller and he was fading in and out like the wires that were hooked up to him weren't monitoring his health, but dimming him like he was a lamp plugged into a light switch.

We were all quiet for a while, then Todd said, "Mom, you've been here for almost twenty-four hours. You need to get something to eat, or move around, or something."

"Like hell," Mom said, "what if he wakes up before the … the …" She couldn't finish what she wanted to say and we all still knew what she meant. I was getting antsy. I could feel the fog pressing on me with all the noises of the hospital egging it on - the sounds of it, the beeping, the hissing, and the smells, too. I knew we had been there for hours. I typed, "Mom, you really should get some food," but when I looked over she was asleep in her chair. Todd smiled at me and looked over at Susie real quick before he asked, "Are you okay, sis? We're going to go down to the cafeteria. Do you want to come, or do you want us to bring you something back?"

I typed, "I'm staying. Just a coffee, please, with lots of cream and lots of sugar."

Todd said, "I know," and squeezed my shoulder as he walked past.

With Mom asleep, I was alone with Dad. I moved my chair closer to his bed so I could hold his hand. The doctors and nurses hadn't hooked anything up to his left hand and I squeezed it. He didn't squeeze back. I looked down at a hand I had held thousands of times, a hand that had pulled me out of the fog too many times to count, a hand that had always been strong and sure, and it lay limp and weak and fading in mine. I brought his hand up to the side of my face hoping that he would stroke my cheek, pushing my hair back away, and tucking it behind my ear like he always did. He didn't. His hand was cold and still in mine. I squeezed his shrinking, fading hand between both of mine to try and warm it up, then I looked around the room again. There was no one there but Mom, still asleep. The room they had put Dad in was at the far end of a long hall, so no one heard me start to talk. I said, "Dad." He still didn't squeeze my hand, or move, or anything.

I tried harder and harder, pushing at the fog, trying to speak like everybody else. I said, "Dad, Dad ple-ase."

Nothing.

The Fog Within

I was quiet on the outside. If a nurse walked in she would have no idea that inside I was screaming at the fog. I was screaming and yelling every bad word I had ever heard my dad or Abby say. I was punching and kicking at the fog, biting and wailing. *Let me do this! Leave me alone and let me do this! If you're a part of me like you always say you are, then God damn it let me do this!...*

...The fog didn't say anything. It was quiet, so I tried to say what I've wanted to for over thirty years and couldn't, at least not with *my* voice. Squeezing hard on Dad's hand, I said, "Dad, please, I love you."

I don't care if you don't believe me. I don't care if you think it was the fog playing one more mean trick in a long line of mean tricks on me. But, I know I said it. That's all that matters. That and I know my daddy heard me say it, because I felt his fingers squeeze back on mine, right before the monitors started beeping real loud and the nurses rushed in, pushing me out of the way.

Mom and I were both pulled out into the hallway while the nurses and doctors rushed about. We hugged each other. We held onto each other real tight as the doctors and nurses shook their heads and stopped working. I looked down at my hand and still felt the tingling from where Dad had squeezed back ... then I started to cry.

Chapter Thirty

The next few days went by in a blur. Todd took care of almost everything. Mom was too upset. She would barely eat or drink anything. She just sat in her bedroom and cried. I stared out the windows most of the time. Not looking at anything that was out there - the houses and yards and people - but looking at what was inside. In my mind I was looking at things that weren't really there. Bobby still lived next door with his dad Jim and the two of them helped Todd out with all the arrangements. I was really glad Bobby was still there. I wasn't doing much better than Mom. I was probably worse in fact, but no one could see it from the outside. The fog may have let me tell Dad that I loved him before he died, but since it had had a moment of weakness it was now rolling back over me with a vengeance. I would be walking through a room of people telling me they were sorry and I'd hear his voice…

… *"Hey there, MC. What's wrong? Why the long face? You're no horse."*…

…I'd turn around real quick, and see him standing in the doorway, holding a cup of coffee and grinning at me. He looked like he always did. He looked like the gentle giant with the spark in his sad eyes, not the fading, weak thing that had been lying in that hospital bed. Then I'd take a step toward him, thinking it had been the fog all along. That he hadn't died, and as soon as I'd reach out toward him the fog would sweep him away, just poof in a gust of nothing and gone. Nobody noticed. I always did odd things anyway, so if they did see me acting strange they just shrugged it off as Megan being Megan.

The fog was relentless. I'd go out front to sit on the porch and be alone. But in minutes I'd hear the rocking chair next to me creak and...

... *"Hey MC, do you need anything? I'm always here for you, kiddo. You know that, right?...*

...I'd look over and he'd be sitting in the chair with his feet propped up on the railing. He'd smile at me, but as soon as I'd move toward him the fog would sweep him away again. I was starting to hate and love the fog at the same time. Hate it still for all that it had done to me, for all it had taken from me, but love it too, because through it I could still see Dad even though he was gone for everybody else. It was torture, but a good torture. I bet Mom would take some of the fog if it meant she could see Dad again as often and as realistically as I was seeing him ... and not some fading, dream-like memory.

I was glad Jim and Bobby could help Todd, because none of them had the fog to distract them. If you're fog-free it would probably be hard to do all the stuff that had to be done after somebody dies. Mom could hide and Todd could do what they needed a family member for, but Jim and Bobby could handle the rest. There really wasn't all that much to do Bobby said. Dad had a will, that's some kind of paper that tells people what a person wants done after they die. I always thought it was a name. I know lots of guys named Will, but then Bobby's dad is Jim and then there's a gym. It must be the same thing with the wills.

Dad's will was simple. No funeral, no flowers, no grave so no headstone, no coffin, no, as Bobby said Dad's will put it, "None of that pomp and ceremony bullshit the rest of the world loves." Which Bobby said some of the guys in ties handling the legal parts of the will couldn't believe Dad had had a bad word typed into it. But Bobby believed it and thought it was funny. He said, "It's just like your dad. All he wanted done is that everybody who wants to is supposed to show up at your old house and have a party. He's being cremated and Todd's going to take care of his remains. Everybody else is just supposed to show up and drink, laugh, and cry for a few days." Bobby chuckled at the idea, but his eyes looked sad.

Dad's death party had another of those confusing words, it was a wake, but I knew Dad was dead. He wouldn't ever be awake again. I didn't want to ask anybody about the words I didn't know like wake, cremation, and remains, because during those blurred days the littlest thing could start anybody crying. A simple question that the fog kept me from understanding could make Mom cry harder, or Todd, or Bobby, or Jim, or Susie, or anyone of all the different people that kept stopping by the house. Dad had a lot of friends. There was no place for people to park. Jim had been letting people park their cars in his back yard, but it was full. People were parking blocks away and walking. It was nice to see. He had meant so much to me, but it was nice that he meant enough to other people that they wanted to come drink and tell stories about him. There were lots of stories I had never heard before from people I had never met, but they were sad and crying that my dad had died, so it was neat too, in a sad way. Bobby and I cried harder when a taxi pulled up along the other side of the street, and Abby climbed out. She helped Ethan get out of the backseat. He was almost as big as we were when Abby and I first met.

I ran out the front door and fell into my friend's arms. We were both crying so hard I think Ethan was scared and he kind of hid behind Abby's legs. Bobby came out behind me and hugged Abby real quick and kissed her on the cheek. He leaned down to Ethan and said, "Hi Ethan, I'm Bobby. We met when you were little. I'm an old friend of your mom's. Do you like video games?"

Ethan nodded, but still looked scared. He looked up at Abby and she said, "Go ahead with Bobby, honey. He'll have more video games than you've ever seen. I'll be here if you need me, but I need to talk to Aunt Megan right now okay, buddy?"

Ethan looked a little less scared and followed Bobby over to his house, so he wouldn't have to watch all the adults around him cry. Most of which he didn't even know. When Bobby's door closed Abby hugged me again and started crying. She said, "I'm so sorry, honey. I can't believe it. I don't want to believe it. When Bobby called, I said, 'No, never Papa Cooper!' and I hung up on him because I thought he was playing a sick joke. When Todd called and said it was true, I lost it. I refused to accept it. I want to walk in that door and hear him say, 'Hey Abs, where you been, kiddo'?"

I cried and didn't type anything. She hugged me and said, "I don't want that just for me. I'm not that selfish, honey. I want that for you. I know what he meant to you." She placed her hand on my cheek and looked me in the eye. Her eyes were sad and tired. They looked like Dad's eyes as she asked, "Is there anything I can do for you?"

I wanted to scream, to yell, and to talk without my stupid talker. I wanted to say, "Yes Abby! You can move back home where you should have been all these years!"

But I didn't.

I shook my head and took Abby's hand. I led her through all the people jammed into my childhood home. I led her past Jim where he was sitting on the couch, taking up half of it. He had a beer in his hand and he kept crying and taking sips. In-between sips he kept saying, to whoever would listen, "If it should have been anybody. It should have been me, not John. Look at me. It isn't fair!"

I wanted to type to him that nothing is fair. Fair is only for people who don't understand the concept. Fair is for *Fairytales*, not real life. But, I didn't. Jim needed his words, whether they made sense or not. His words were helping him through his pain, just like the fog was helping me through mine.

I led Abby back to my parents' room, where Mom was doing her best to hide from all the people that were there to say goodbye to Dad. I think she thought if she didn't say goodbye like they were then it wasn't over. I don't think she wanted to believe the spark was gone either, just like Abby, and just like me. She had her back to the door when I opened it, and she didn't turn around at the door's squeak. She held up her left hand like she didn't want us to come any further. She was probably tired of people telling her they were sorry. I know I was. I didn't want people to be sorry. I wanted my dad back. I wanted people to be happy like my Happy – who was curled up in my old bedroom purring away on my old bed, completely happy to be there and completely unconcerned with all the sadness around him. To Mom's back I said, "Mum."

She turned around and when she saw Abby she got up so fast she knocked her chair over. She hugged Abby as hard as she could and they both cried. I backed out of the room and shut the door. The other people in the house didn't need to hear them crying.

I didn't want to wander around and listen to more people I didn't know tell me they were sorry, so I went to my room where I could pet Happy. He jumped down from my bed when I opened the door and ran over so he could rub against my leg. I picked him up and sat down on my old bed...

... *"Happy, huh? I still think you should've gone with Mooch."* ...

...I looked over at my squished beanbag chair and Dad was sitting in it with his hands behind his head. He smiled at me and I smiled back. He winked but the fog swept him away again before I could wink back. I sat in my room for hours petting Happy until I could hear people starting to leave. I could hear car doors shut and engines start. My room was getting darker but I didn't want to turn the light on. I wanted to sit on my old bed and feel my happy cat Happy purr as I petted him. When it was completely dark my door opened and Abby came in. She had a beer in one hand and she sat down on the bed next to me just like she used to when we were kids ... well except for the beer.

She didn't say anything and for a long time she sat there next to me, occasionally taking sips from her beer. After a while she reached over and scratched Happy behind his ears. It was the first time he noticed that somebody else was in the room. He got up from my lap and moved over to Abby and started to purr while she petted him. She asked, "Did you finally name the little guy?"

I typed, "Yes, his name is Happy."

Abby laughed and said, "That's a great name, Megan. You figured out who he was alright. He is a happy little thing isn't he?" Happy had rolled over so Abby would scratch his stomach and he purred louder when she did.

"Yeah," I said and we were silent again. There was nothing to say, or type, was there? She was going to leave soon – if not that night, then the next day for sure. We were all going to go back to our lives, go back to doing the same things, and pretend like everything was normal. That's all we ever do isn't it, just pretend? Everything is okay. Everything is fine if you just pretend that it is.

Abby and Ethan stayed the night in Todd's old bedroom, but as fast as she had been swept back into my life, she was swept just as fast right back out. She had a job to get back to and Ethan had to get back for school. It was good to see them again. It was good to see her again, but it made me sad the next morning when they rode off in a taxi to know that I had gotten my wish - that I had seen my friend again, but at the price of losing my dad. I know my wish didn't cause my dad to die. I'm not stupid remember, just crazy. But it made me sad that I had

216

wished for something silly, something like seeing Abby again, when I should have wished that I'd have my daddy for a while longer. It's silly and childish to wish for anything. Who's going to grant those wishes, and how, by magic? But ... but sometimes wishing is all we have, better to wish for the impossible and still have hope, than to never wish at all and believe things will always turn out bad ... sometimes it's better to just pretend.

Chapter Thirty-one

How do you go back to life after somebody close to you dies? Everybody has to do it. Everybody has to go back to doing things like they did before the person they loved died: go to work, go to school, go to the store, eat, sleep, and everything else. You know the drill. You do it every day, but once someone that was a big part of that drill is gone it's one of the hardest things we have to do I think.

I dealt with it better than most people do. Of course everybody thought that was because I didn't understand. I heard it over and over. "Poor Megan, she doesn't really understand what happened. She's special you know. She doesn't understand her dad is gone." Or some other version of that when people thought that I wasn't listening.

Of course I understood what had happened. It's just that the fog had taken so much from me my whole life. It had taken most of my childhood in one big sweeping haze of emotions. It had taken my teen years in a wave of misunderstanding. I was used to the fog taking things from me. I was used to loss. I was used to moving on. I didn't want to. I didn't want to go back to doing all those things in a world without my dad. But … he was one more loss in a life of losses. He wouldn't have wanted me to fall apart like Mom. He would have wanted me to help her.

I moved back into my old house. I don't remember when it was decided, who decided it, or if it was one of those things that happen because everybody knows it's the right thing to do, but no one actually says it aloud. Once Happy and I stayed for Dad's wake, we didn't leave. Todd and Bobby went to my apartment and got most of my stuff in a couple of trips with Bobby's truck. It was like I had never moved out. My social worker Betty said I didn't have to go back to work at the zoo ... but I asked her why would I want to stop going to work? If I didn't go and take people's tickets I'd end up going anyway and looking at the animals all day. It would be better to go and work for a few hours than go just to visit. I liked my job, and Dad wouldn't have wanted me to stop doing something I liked because he was gone. I may not know much about what the rest of the world does. I may not be the smartest person you'll ever meet. But, I know you shouldn't stop doing something you love just because you lost someone you loved.

My mom didn't go back to work. She took an early retirement. I guess Todd had written out policies on all of us. I asked what the policies were and he said that if one of us died, like Dad had, then the rest of us would get a bunch of money, so they didn't have to work for a while if they didn't want to, or if they were too sad to, like Mom was. I typed,

"That's weird, Todd. Mom gets money because Dad died? Why?"

He told me it was insurance and not to worry about it … but I still didn't like it. I was happy Mom could stay home and be sad if she needed to be, without having to worry about going to work, but I think if she went to work like I did it might help her not be as sad. I also didn't like the idea that people got money from a policy when somebody died. That seemed wrong. It made me worry that other people would try to hurt people for money. I tried to type some of that, but Todd said, "It's okay, Megan, really. Lots of people have insurance policies for if they die suddenly like Dad did. It makes them feel good to know if something happens the people they love are taken care of."

I still didn't like it, but I figured it was one of those office, ties, and reports type things that the rest of the adult world is always worrying about. One of those things that only makes sense to people without the fog. One of those things that I was better off not bothering with because it would never make sense – like obeying ticking black lines on a clock as a kid.

We do things to get Mom out of the house. Todd and Susie say it's to help her move past it. I take her out for pizza … well she still has to drive, but we go out and I pay! I don't think me trying to learn to drive would help her not be so sad. I think it might scare her more, so if we go anywhere she drives. I still walk a few blocks and take the bus to work. I think she feels better since she doesn't have to go to work at night anymore, not like a raccoon, but I also think she feels about it how I do about seeing Abby again – that it wasn't worth it, that she'd work forever at night if it would bring Dad back. Happy's been good for her too. When she's really sad he follows her around the house, purring until she stops and pets him.

The only difference at home and work for me is that I can't watch the fish anymore. If I stop at the huge aquarium at work, all I see are fish waiting to die, not fish being fish. I see them as glazed-eyed and ready to be flushed down a toilet. I see Dad as he was at the end, lying in a big hospital bed, shrinking and fading. I didn't want my fish to just die, but I couldn't stand looking at them, so I asked Bobby if he'd adopt them for me. He said yes without wanting an explanation. He said, "If you need anything, Megan, anything at all, just let me know. I'm right here, right next door again, so don't hesitate, okay?"

He sounded so much like my dad when he said that it made the fog push Dad's eyes onto Bobby's. It was sad to see the same tired look again, especially from my friend.

The Fog Within

Chapter Thirty-two

Months passed and the seasons changed – warm to cold and back to warm again. Happy grew from a kitten into a big fat cat. He turned out to be weird for a cat. I liked that. Happy enjoyed walking on a leash, even though the largest harness I could find still looked tiny on him. His fat black belly hung low every evening when I'd take Happy for a walk around our neighborhood. All of the houses have their back yards up against a sort of shared forest, and Happy loved to smell the different wild animal smells that would come from the forest: squirrels, raccoons, opossums, skunks, foxes, chipmunks, and all the other animals you have in an in town forest.

After Happy's walk we'd sit out on the back porch with Mom. Some days there'd be an extra beer waiting for me, and some days it would be a cup of coffee. We didn't drink coffee too often, because it made us both think about Dad. Sometimes that was okay; sometimes we wanted to think about him … but others? Other nights we wanted to think about what we had going on then and not what we had in the past. If it was a beer night, I'd tell Mom about my day at the zoo: what animals did what, which ones might have babies, which ones did have babies, which ones were getting new fake rocks or plastic plants, and other zoo talk.

Mom had decided to go back to work, but she didn't do what she used to. She said, "Your father wouldn't want me sulking around here forever, Megan. If I don't go do something he'll probably send a ghost to come haunt me. He won't come himself. He knows that's what I'd want, so he'd send somebody to annoy me, like the ghost of Buddy Hackett or something." So Mom had gone to work for a daycare. She liked working with all the little kids. She said she was getting to do some of the things she'd missed out on while she worked nights when Todd and I were the age of the kids she helped take care of. I was glad Mom had found something to make her happy again. I still found her crying sometimes when she was looking at old pictures or if she found something of Dad's that we'd kept, but those times happened less and less as the weather kept changing and changing.

Sometimes when we'd sit out back with Happy playing in the grass, Bobby would come over and have a beer with us ... or a coffee, if it was a remember Dad night. Jim would always wave and say hi or talk, but he couldn't handle the sit down and talk about the past nights. He'd start crying and Bobby would get embarrassed, so Jim usually stayed home. I understood. Jim didn't have many friends, just like I didn't as a kid, so Dad was to Jim what Abby had been to me. I don't know what's worse; losing a parent or losing a friend. I guess they both hurt, so there shouldn't be any comparison.

The Fog Within

One evening when the weather was getting really warm, Bobby came over and sat down with us. None of us said anything. We sat and drank our beer – I was only allowed one a night because of some of my old pills, new pills, red pills, blue pills. We watched Happy chase a butterfly. He'd catch it, then let it go, then he'd catch it again. He was on a leash, tied to the porch, in his own cage like the lions, but he still wasn't sad about it. When the butterfly flew past the length that his leash would let him reach, he watched it go but not with sad lion eyes. No, he watched it fly away with happy content eyes. The fog whispered…

…He's only happy, Megan, because he doesn't know any better. He doesn't know that the butterfly is flying away forever. He thinks the butterfly will come back when he wants to play with it. That is if he ever thinks about the butterfly again at all…

…The fog was right. I hated it, but it was right. My mom must have felt some of what I was thinking because she said, "I'm switching to coffee you guys. I'm going to go brew a pot. Hey Bobby, how about you and Megan go for a walk and you can show her the … well whatever it is you want to call it. I think she'll like it. I'll take Happy inside with me and the coffee should be ready by the time you get back."

I looked back and forth between them. Mom smiled, but Bobby looked a little nervous. I typed, "Show me what thing?"

Mom scooped up Happy in one hand and our empty beer bottles in the other. She said, "Oh it's just something Bobby made for you. It's very nice, but I don't want to ruin the surprise, so I'll just..." She kept talking as she went into the house and I couldn't hear her. Bobby stood up and held out his hand. In the nervous Bobby voice that always made me think of high school, he said, "Please, Megan ... I ... I've been working on it for a long time now and I think it's ready. But I want to talk to you first." He stopped for a breath but still held his hand out when he continued, "So please, let's take a walk?"

Chapter Thirty-three

Bobby and I walked that slow shuffle walk you see old people do in parks and at grocery stores sometimes. It's the walk of people with no need to move faster, no need to do anything but shuffle along. The fog would typically hate that kind of walking, but Bobby held my hand and squeezed it every now and then while he talked, so I focused on that instead of the fog whispering.

Bobby started talking like he had something he wanted to say and he needed to say it fast. It was like what he had to say hurt, like ripping off a band aide, so he wanted to do it quickly. He said. "I miss your dad, Megan. I miss him a lot. You know how much I looked up to him as a kid. He was everything I wanted my dad to be. I love my dad and he and I have gotten over all that stupid, bullshit teenage angst that high school places on every kid, and now we're pretty good friends. We even work really well together which isn't something most people can do when they're family."

I didn't try to type anything into my talker. I just walked, listened, and held his hand. I could hear the pain in his voice. Sometimes the best thing you can say when you hear pain in your friend's voice is nothing at all. Let them say their pain, and get rid of it. Bobby continued, "I loved your dad. He was my

226

friend. He was the only adult that didn't treat me like every other kid and talk down to me. He treated me like an adult and he didn't pretend like I was some psycho because I liked to play video games and not sports. He treated me like I was a person with an opinion worth listening to. He was my friend and I miss him damn it."

I squeezed Bobby's hand to let him know I understood. He squeezed my hand back. We had shuffled around our neighborhood once and started on another lap when he said, "One day, years ago your dad caught me working on what I want to show you. I was so scared. I must have been about ten or eleven. I thought, 'Oh God, Mr. Cooper is going to kill me for this!' but that was when I realized your dad was my friend. He looked at what I was doing and he smiled. He shook his head and said, 'Alright kid, I figured as much, but I was hoping you'd keep your feelings to yourself a bit longer, pal. How about we keep this between you and me for now, huh Bobby my boy? What do you say?' And he held his hand out for me to shake like I was an adult and not some stupid kid playing out in the woods."

Bobby shook his head and laughed at the memory. I could see Dad in my mind, leaning down to shake a scared young Bobby's hand and I laughed a little too. Bobby laughed even harder and asked, "Remember that time at the zoo when I said I'd take you to prom?"

I nodded and smiled. Bobby kept laughing as he said, "As soon as we walked away from all of you guys, your dad said, 'You can speak whenever you want, kid. I don't care, just if you wouldn't mind trying to keep up the whole *speak* when I tell you to thing in front of the rest of them – especially my wife – I'd love to mess with them like that.' I said I would and I felt better because at first I thought he was going to kill me. I really did, just like when I was little and he caught me in the woods ... but again he surprised me. He said, 'I can't think of a better person to take Megan to prom. I know you're in love with her son. I've known that since I saw you out by that tree, but again Bobby, just like then, I need to ask you to hold onto that. She isn't ready. I'm not ready. And to tell you the truth my friend I don't know if she'll ever be ready.' He stopped and looked at me. I mean *looked* at me. I was too scared to look away, but he put a hand on my shoulder and said, 'I know she's going to need somebody to look out for her someday, because I won't always be there. Todd will do what he can, but he'll have his own life. Abs has a good heart but she can barely take care of herself. You never know what the future is going to hold Bobby. So if somebody has to look out for her, I'd be proud if it was you.' I about threw up."

Then looking over at me quickly he added, "Not at the thought of looking out for you, Megan, but at the thought that he'd be willing to give me that kind of responsibility. That he'd treat a seventeen year old boy like a man. That was why I was so nervous and scared around prom that year, not because of your dad, but because of the level he was willing to trust me. I didn't want to let him down."

We had stopped shuffle walking in front of Bobby's house and he pulled on my hand to get me to follow him around to the backyard. It was getting close to night and the forest behind our houses was darkening with shadows. There was a small path Bobby had worn into the weeds and thorns. I followed him as he walked into the woods. I wanted to ask him what we were doing, but I trusted my friend. If Dad trusted him – I trusted him. The small path ended around a tall pine tree that was clear of underbrush and stood by itself in the middle of the woods behind our houses.

Bobby moved off to one side and looked at his feet like he did when he was an embarrassed kid. He sounded like he was apologizing when he started to talk. "I … I know it might be silly, even when I first started it. I knew it was weird when I started to use my dad's ladder to reach the higher branches … but, I remembered what you had told me about everybody being weird and I thought what the hell, be weird Bobby. You're doing it for the girl you love. What better time than to be weird than out of love?"

I looked at the pine tree. It had hundreds of spoons hanging from its branches – more than hundreds, thousands, maybe tens of thousands. I stood there lost for a moment. The fog didn't whisper. The fog didn't say or do anything. I think it was in as much shock and wonder as I was. Every spoon I had ever thrown out of my parents' window or taken out to the backyard and hurled into these woods was hanging from the pine tree. It was beautiful and sad and weird and amazing all at the same time. Bobby said, "I hadn't worked on it for years. I had it maybe halfway done when you moved out and I kind of figured it would be one of those projects you start and just never finish. But then … but then when your dad died, I thought it would be just as much of a memorial to him as it would be to you. I know you're the one who threw all those spoons out, Megan. Hell, I watched you do it half of the time. But I tell you, as I was putting the last of them up toward the top I could have sworn I heard your dad laughing. I could have sworn I saw his face in the reflections on the backs of some of them. I know it sounds crazy … I … I'm sorry, Megan, but it feels like he's here for me. Like I have my friend back. I don't mean to sound creepy or weird, but I wanted to share it with you."

I didn't say anything. I walked over closer to the tree and touched a spoon. It dangled and swayed like a Christmas ornament. When it stopped moving I didn't see my reflection in it. I saw my dad. I saw him as he was when I was real little. He looked so young, too young to be so sad. He was younger than I was when I looked at the spoon. Then I looked at a few more and I saw him in different places and at different points in his life. He was sad, he was happy, he was dancing with Mom, he was holding little Tahbey out to me and smiling. He was in every spoon. The fog whispered...

...No he's not, Megan. He's dead. He's gone. Don't be like your silly cat and pretend that he flew away and he'll come back when you need him. He is gone...

...But he wasn't. He was standing behind me. I could see his reflection in the spoon I was staring at. He was smiling and laughing. No, that was Bobby. Bobby was standing behind me, not my dad. I could see his reflection overlay Dad's in all the spoons as he reached his arms out and hugged me from behind. I leaned back into Bobby's arms. I closed my hands on his, and squeezed as I closed my eyes to help quiet the fog.

Author's Notes II

Hello again reader. Well, I have so much to say I almost don't know where to start. I want to thank you for reading what has undoubtedly been the hardest book I have written to date, and though I have some other emotional novels on the horizon, I doubt they will twist me about so much as *The Fog Within* has.

I'd like to point out that although I based much of this work on my daughter and our interaction with the world, I don't want you for a second to think that Megan's school experiences were my daughter's. I have dealt with so many caring individuals in the education system, both paid and volunteer, that I wouldn't want you to think poorly of them. But I have heard many horror stories from other parents and I did my best to make a compromise, to make the staff of Megan's elementary school human, meaning fallible and capable of distraction like the rest of us.

Part one of the story as a whole was very difficult for me because that is what I am living with at the moment, where Megan is lost the furthest in the fog. The entire work parallels my life: Part one: Childhood is my reality. Part two: Adolescence is my hopes and fears, and Part three: Adulthood is the scariest of all – the unknown, or to be more precise,

232

what we all struggle with in adulthood; not cultural concepts like mortgages, 401ks, and Social Security, but the more important battle – our own mortality.

The narrative itself was an absolute nightmare. If you have read any of my other novels you are familiar with how deep I go into my character's psyche. When I write as any of my characters, for a time I become them (We're all weird. Everybody is weird. We just pretend that we aren't). I see the world through their eyes and I tell the story how I feel it would be for them true to form, to idea, and to speech patterns. Even if, as was the case with *The Fog Within*, when I had to use redundant phrasing and repetitive language, my inner editor was screaming the entire time (oddly enough in an English accent, my editor voice sounds very similar to John Cleese), "Damn it man! Use a bloody synonym!"

But the thing was (Cleese-like ranting voice aside) Megan would not know to use synonyms. Words confuse her as it is. She would use the simplest words, with the most direct meaning over and over again to get her point across. So when I was in her mind, when I was writing as Megan I felt I could never use too, too often, because she wouldn't bother saying also or as well. She wouldn't care how many times she said, "Too." It could be one, two, three, four, or five – Five! times and she wouldn't care. I had to be true to character no matter the cost to grammar, punctuation, or sentence structure.

The differing severity of autism, of the spectrum as it is called, never ceases to boggle my mind. Yet, I have run into it time and again, where some medical personnel will say to a parent, "That's just autism," when said parent is describing their child's newest and oddest behavior that has the family locked away, prisoners in their own home because they are afraid of what people will think of their child if they were to take them out in public. God have I been there. If you're one of the spectrum parents who have been brushed off by the ever so popular, "That's just autism," excuse I want you to know you aren't alone. You also aren't alone in wanting to wrap your fingers around that medical practitioner's throat and shake them until different, more compassionate words come out, like maybe, "Sorry, it must be difficult. I'm not sure where to go from here, but let's run some tests and make some referrals, okay?"

That's just autism. Come on, really? That's like an oncologist walking into a patient's room and saying, "Hey there, I just scraped off this tiny stage one melanoma from this fat guy's ass! But you know what? From my perspective since I don't currently have cancer myself and I don't really care, I basically see it as the same thing as your stage four lymphoma. Cool huh?"

No, any umbrella/spectrum disorder deserves the respect of any mental illness. Degree of severity can all be a matter of perspective, and perspective always changes when you slip into someone else's shoes. It's something everybody should do more often and this world would be a better place for all of us if we did. Those of us lost in the fog and those of us who are lucky enough to not be.

I want to leave you with a side story. A true account that I have told before in articles and at speaking engagements, so some of you may have already heard or read it. But I don't believe there is a better way to sum up my notes on living with autism than a little piece of non-fiction, a small snippet of my unwritten autobiography that I like to call – *Rainbows and Rocks.*

In the spring after my daughter was diagnosed with autism we lived close by to a community park that had very elaborate, manicured gardens. Paige would run around, grabbing or squeezing the flowers, and typically my job was to stop her from ruining the garden. It was exhausting to follow her every step, to have to treat a three and a half year old like a destructive eighteen month old. Most times we'd visit at odd hours so if I didn't get to her fast enough and she ripped the head off of a daisy or petunia, I didn't have to hear the tsks and sighs of some old biddy complaining that I couldn't control my child. After years the tsks and sighs tend to

235

weigh you down and pull you under the waters of bitterness.

So I'd take Paige to the gardens when other people were busy going about their normal lives, while she and I not only danced to the beat of a different drummer, but a whole dissimilar orchestra.

One evening a spring thunderstorm had passed through and we lived so close to the park that I knew if we left right away, Paige and I could have the park to ourselves for at least a half an hour before anybody else would wander out-of-doors as the black clouds rolled out of the way for navy blue, dusky skies. We wandered for a bit and Paige decided she wanted to sit down and play with some rocks by a wide-open field, hedged in bright red rose bushes. I didn't care. If she was playing with rocks I didn't have to run defense for the flowers. So I let her sit and play, picking up large and small rocks and putting them back down. It was nice and quiet at the park. It's amazing how much a few moments of silence can help you as you age. Kids whine, yell, talk, scream, cry, and sometimes all within the same minute. The older I get the more I value silence. The park was silent but for a few birds chirping as the sun shone out from fluffy white clouds that were pushing their dark predecessors away. I could feel the warmth on my face and I closed my eyes.

Then the moment was over. I heard a little boy's high-pitched, shrieking voice, "Mommy look it! Look it! A rainbow!"

I opened my eyes to see that the *Family Circus* had wandered off the pages of the Funnies and had now joined Paige and me at the gardens. The youngest boy was about the same age as my daughter that couldn't or wouldn't speak. He was running circles around his family shouting about the rainbow as he went, "Daddy rainbow! Tammy-Sue rainbow! Jimmy rainbow! Sparky, look it, a rainbow!"

To his credit it was a spectacular rainbow, a full arch, end to end touching the horizon and shining brighter than any rainbow I can ever remember witnessing. I crouched down and tried to get Paige's attention. I said, "Look kiddo, do you see the rainbow?" I tried to point it out to her. I tried to show her. There's no point in pushing an autistic child's head in the direction you want them to face. Some doctors can feel free to disagree with me on that, but I've yet to see the case where the child does not begrudge the action and refuse to cooperate more so. I let Paige clack and clank her rocks together. I'll be honest, that was one of the lowest moments of my life. I don't have some mental VH1 countdown Top Ten Nick's Shittiest Moments, or anything, but that moment would be on there if I did, believe you me. I wanted to scream. Not at anybody in particular, not at Paige, not at the little boy and his *Family Circus*, but at the rainbow. I wanted to scream at the sky, "Fuck you! Is this what my life is going to be like? Is this what her life is going to be like? Passing us both by, with one of us looking in and the other looking out, but neither being a part of things? Is it?"

But as I mentally accosted the sky I heard a shriek of pain and agony. I looked over to see that the little boy had been so preoccupied with the rainbow that in his excitement he had run headlong into the rosebush hedge, and was stuck screaming and crying as his parents tried to untangle him. I looked down at Paige where she sat by my feet playing with her rocks. She looked up and held her rocks out for me to see. I nodded wide-eyed and said, "Yeah, those are cool!"

I laughed, not out of any sadistic cruelty at the little boy's accident, but at the realization that would carry me through the rest of my life. The realization that would keep me grounded more often than not and keep me from screaming at the sky. The realization that life gives you rainbows, and life gives you rocks. It's up to you to watch where you are going.

Thank you for reading. I wish you the best in life, be you given rainbows or rocks, make the most of them.

Cheers!

Nick Shamhart

About the Author

Nick Shamhart was born in Sandusky, Ohio on the winter solstice in the years before Americans started electing actors as President. He still lives in that mostly vowel state under protest from half of the voices in his head. The other half could care less where they reside, because they are too busy yammering on endlessly about everything from Sit-Com theme songs to theology and metaphysics.

Nick Shamhart is not a genre writer. His novels are character based. The result is whatever the story becomes, from romantic comedy to drama or thriller. He is the author of the theologically and psychologically driven series based on the afterlife called the Balance Books. The romantic comedy, "The Knight's Wife" is based on the concept of how often women are actually the ones who perform the hero's work and then some. "The Fog Within" is Nick's bestselling and highly acclaimed dramatic look into the mind of a severely autistic woman. He lives in Cleveland with his wife and two daughters.

<u>Books by Nick Shamhart</u>

The Balance Series:

Grey (Book One)

Raven (Book Two)

Zeus (Book Three)

Gabe (Book Four)

<u>Others</u>

The Knight's Wife

The Fog Within